Aliens, Underwear, and Monsters

SIXTH-GRADE ALIEN

Previously titled
There's an Alien in My Underwear

Aliens, Underwear, and Monsters

By **BRUCE COVILLE**

Illustrated by Glen Mullaly

ALADDIN

NEW YORK   LONDON   TORONTO   SYDNEY   NEW DELHI

ALADDIN

An imprint of Simon & Schuster Children's Publishing Division

1230 Avenue of the Americas, New York, New York 10020

This Aladdin hardcover edition January 2022

Text copyright © 2001, 2022 by Bruce Coville

Previously published in 2001 as *There's an Alien in My Underwear*

Illustrations copyright © 2022 by Glen Mullaly

Also available in an Aladdin paperback edition.

All rights reserved, including the right of reproduction in whole or in part in any form.

ALADDIN and related logo are registered trademarks of Simon & Schuster, Inc.

For information about special discounts for bulk purchases, please contact Simon & Schuster Special Sales at 1-866-506-1949 or business@simonandschuster.com.

The Simon & Schuster Speakers Bureau can bring authors to your live event. For more information or to book an event contact the Simon & Schuster Speakers Bureau at 1-866-248-3049 or visit our website at www.simonspeakers.com.

Designed by Tiara Iandiorio

The illustrations for this book were rendered in a mix of traditional and digital media.

The text of this book was set in Noyh Book.

Manufactured in the United States of America 1221 FFG

2 4 6 8 10 9 7 5 3 1

Library of Congress Control Number 2021941095

ISBN 9781534487376 (hc)

ISBN 9781534487369 (pbk)

ISBN 9781534487383 (ebook)

FOR MARIA SANSEVERO,
MOST BEAUTIFUL DENTIST ON
THE PLANET
AND
SOURCE OF MORE WEIRD
CREATURES THAN YOU WOULD
EVER GUESS

CONTENTS

CHAPTER 1

[TIM]
KOO MUK DWAN

"So, how's it going with Jordan?" asked Rafaella Martinez.

The two of us, Rafaella and I, had stopped our bikes and were standing side by side on the bridge we cross on the way home from school. I love the bridge because it gives a great view of the Hevi-Hevian embassy, which is located on top of the big hill in Thorncraft Park. The embassy looks a lot like a huge flying saucer. It dangles from a two-hundred-foot-high hook that arches up from the hill like the top of a coat hanger. The hook is made from some alien metal. It's only about a foot wide, and looks incredibly flimsy for something so huge.

Bruce Coville

No matter how often I see the embassy, I don't get tired of it. How could I? My whole life I had been wanting to meet an alien. So when our teacher, Ms. Weintraub, announced that the first alien embassy on Earth was going to be put here in Syracuse, I thought my head would explode. It's a good thing I didn't find out *then* that Pleskit, the alien ambassador's son and world's first purple sixth grader, would turn out to be my best friend. I think the excitement would have killed me on the spot!

Today, as usual, a crowd of sightseers was gathered below the embassy, gawking up at it. I knew most of them would give their right arms to get inside, so I couldn't help but feel slightly smug about the fact that I visit it almost daily.

"Big crowd this afternoon," I said.

Rafaella nudged me with her elbow. "Stop avoiding my question!"

She was right, of course; that was exactly what I was doing. But it was a tricky subject. Jordan Lynch had been my mortal enemy ever since he'd transferred into our school two years before, after he'd gotten kicked out of the fancy private school he used to go to. But

Aliens, Underwear, and Monsters

things had started to change after Jordan, Pleskit, and I had been shrunk by an evil hamsteroid alien named Wiktor-waktor-wooktor. Wiktor wanted to get revenge on us for the fact that Pleskit and I had thwarted the plans of his littersister, Mikta-makta-mookta. Surviving the experience together had changed things between Jordan and me. Only, I still hadn't figured out exactly what the change was.

"I don't know *what* to think," I said to Rafaella at last. "Jordan still isn't what you would call a friend." I shuddered. "I can't imagine that ever happening! But he's definitely not as much of an enemy as he used to be. It's very confusing."

"Don't worry," said Rafaella soothingly. "You'll figure it out eventually."

I smiled. I used to get my social advice from my upstairs neighbor Linnsy Vanderhof, until she got merged into a symbiotic link with a crablike creature named Bur. Now she's off exploring the galaxy. I miss her, and not just because I need her advice—which was often accompanied by a "little punchie-wunchie" in the arm, which was meant to teach me not to be such a dork.

Bruce Coville

To tell the truth, I don't actually miss the punchie-wunchies. But the social advice is something I still desperately need, since I don't have much ability in that direction myself. Fortunately, Rafaella has started helping me with it during the last month or so.

Sometimes I feel guilty about starting to be such good friends with Rafaella, almost as if I were being disloyal to Linnsy in some way. I don't know why I should feel like that, especially since Rafaella is nicer to me than Linnsy ever was. But as my mother always says, "The heart has reasons of which reason knows not." As near as I can make out, this basically means that emotions don't always make sense. Based on personal experience, I would say this is definitely true.

"What *I'm* worried about," said Rafaella, changing the subject slightly, "is Doris. Do you think she's still running around loose in the walls?"

"I'm afraid so," I said uneasily.

Doris used to be one of our class's pet hamsters. We had three of them—Doris the Delightful, Hubert Hugecheeks, and Ronald Roundbutt. But a combination of Pleskit's mega-vitamins and Wiktor-waktor-wooktor's HAMSTER (Human Attribute Maximization,

4

Aliens, Underwear, and Monsters

Strength Treatment, and Energy Raising) Ray had transformed them into intelligent mutants. It turned out Doris had been misnamed; she was anything but delightful.

After Wiktor was captured, each of the mutants chose a different fate. Hubert asked to be turned back into a normal hamster; he was still living in our classroom, happily cramming his face so full of seeds we were always afraid his cheeks were going to burst. Ronald, on the other hand, had gone to live in the Hevi-Hevian embassy—probably the safest place for a miniature mutant, since Earth is not really set up for five-inch-high intelligent beings. As for Doris, she had disappeared into the walls of the school, where she was still lurking, if she hadn't died or reverted. Now whenever anything small disappeared—pencils, erasers, things like that—people blamed it on the renegade hamster.

I was pretty nervous about her. Everyone was, in fact.

The school had put out mousetraps, but the mutated Doris was far too intelligent to fall for anything that simple. They gave up on the traps after they found one where Doris had taken out the bait and replaced it with a picture of Mr. Grand, the school principal. When the janitor took the trap to Mr. Grand, he tried to take out the picture, but the trap snapped shut on him and almost broke his finger. Somehow Doris had made the spring more powerful.

She is not someone to mess with.

Remembering my final battle with Doris made me remember something else. "Holy cow!" I cried. "I've got to get going. McNally promised to give me another Koo Muk Dwan lesson today!"

Rafaella smiled. "You enjoy those, don't you?"

I nodded. "McNally's pretty cool."

McNally — his full name is Robert McNally, but he prefers to be called by just his last name — is Pleskit's Earthling bodyguard. Recently he started teaching me the martial art he was trained in, mostly so I could stop worrying so much about Jordan. It's great! For the first time in my life, I'm starting to feel as if I can take care of myself.

"See you tomorrow," said Rafaella, getting back onto her bike.

As I watched her ride away, I wondered why it bothered me so much to have her go. Then I sighed and hurried off to the embassy to meet my *geeba-raku*.

Aliens, Underwear, and Monsters

(That's what you call your teacher in Koo Muk Dwan.)

McNally was waiting for me, already dressed in his black robes.

"You really love this stuff, don't you?" I asked as we started our session. Well, not exactly as we started. First we had to do breathing exercises, then sit in silence for several minutes to clear our minds, which is probably a good idea, except whenever I sit in silence, my mind just sort of runs berserk.

"It saved my life," said McNally. "Twice."

"You mean because you used it to beat off someone who was trying to kill you?" I asked excitedly.

He shook his head. "No, it saved my life when I was a kid. I was this totally dweeby little guy and —"

"Are you kidding?" I interrupted.

"I don't kid about this stuff, Tim," he said sincerely.

I looked at him in astonishment. It was hard to believe this big, buff bodyguard had been a dweeby little kid once. Maybe there was hope for me after all.

"What I was going to say," continued McNally, "was that Koo Muk Dwan saved me the first time by giving me enough confidence that other kids just stopped picking on me."

He moved into the training posture called "Leg of an Ostrich."

"And the second time?" I asked, imitating him carefully.

"It kept me from getting *too* cool," he said. "I almost got hooked up with the wrong group of kids when I was a teenager. My *geeba-raku* gave me a choice — I could run with them, or study with him. I finally chose to stay with him." He shook his head. "There were about ten guys in that group. By the time we were twenty-one, three of them were dead, and three were in the slammer. Who knows where I'd be now if I hadn't had the right teacher?"

I was listening to this with such astonishment that I forgot to breathe properly, and fell over while I was attempting to move into the pose called "the Giraffe's Elbow."

"How come Pleskit doesn't want to learn this?" I asked.

McNally shrugged. "Hevi-Hevians aren't very interested in the martial arts. I think they believe their civilization has gotten past the need for fighting." He looked at me carefully. "Can you tell me what's wrong with that idea?"

Aliens, Underwear, and Monsters

"This isn't about fighting," I answered quickly, repeating what he had taught me. "It's about mastering your body."

McNally smiled and then spun through a blazing series of leaps.

Man, do I want to be like him when I grow up.

The training session was good but exhausting. My muscles ached as I rode home, but I didn't mind.

Mom was still at the hospital when I got into the apartment. She works as a nurse in the emergency ward, which means she has great stories to tell, really gory things about missing toes and stuff. It took me a while to learn that you can't talk about that kind of thing when other people are at dinner, 'cause it makes them kind of sick. But since Mom has to deal with it every day, it doesn't bother her much.

In the living room I stopped to examine the model of the *Tarbox Moon Warriors* ship that Mom had given me for my birthday. It was an original, from way back when the show first ran, and when I'd opened it, I had been amazed because I know how expensive they are — expensive and just about impossible to get.

"I didn't buy it, Tim," she'd said, smiling. "It belonged to your father. I always intended to give it to you when you turned twelve."

"You are beautiful," I whispered now, stroking the little ship with my fingertip.

Then I grabbed a snack and headed for my room.

When I walked through my bedroom door, I saw something that startled me so much, I nearly dropped my nachos.

CHAPTER 2

[PLESKIT]

THE INTERDIMENSIONAL CAMERA

I was sitting in the embassy lab, deep in thought, when a little voice said, "What'cha doin'?"

The question came from somewhere near my ankle.

Glancing down, I saw Ronald the mutant hamster staring up at me. Ronald is slightly larger than a normal hamster—five or six inches tall—and his arms and legs have grown so that he is shaped like a miniature human. His face, however, is still quite hamsterish. He was wearing a traditional Hevi-Hevian outfit that Shhh-foop, our Queen of the Kitchen, had made for him in her spare time. Shhh-foop is not only a wondrous cook; she is a true artist in all the domestic skills.

11

"What'cha doin'?" he asked again.

"Working on a science project," I replied.

Ronald scratched his head. "I thought the school already had a science fair this year."

"It sure did," I said ruefully, remembering how I had accidentally turned Tim into a zombie while I'd been trying to come up with a project for that event. "But this work isn't for school—at least, not exactly. One of the problems with going to school here is that Earth science is so far behind ours that the Fatherly One has become concerned I will grow deficient in my scientific studies."

"That is thoughtful of him," said Ronald.

"Depends on how you look at it," I said, a trifle bitterly. "Remember, he was the one who dragged me to this backward planet to begin with—not to mention the one who insisted I go to a regular school. However, he is an adult, and I have learned that adults are not always consistent. Anyway, I have decided to do some work on my own. So I'm studying the *Big Book of Science Projects*."

"I don't see a book," said Ronald.

Ronald is very interested in books. He had watched

us reading in school, of course, back when he was an ordinary hamster, but he says he never understood why we found books so interesting, since we didn't eat them. But after his mutation he began learning to read. He became so enthusiastic about it that we used the embassy's computer and printing systems to make him some tiny books just the right size for his paws.

"Well, this isn't really a book," I admitted. "Not like the ones you have. It's all contained in the computer."

"Can I see?" asked Ronald.

I reached down and picked him up so he could stand on the lab table.

"What's this?" he asked, pointing to the display on the monitor.

"Plans for a flying propeller beanie. I can't use one myself, because of my *sphen-gnut-ksher*. I was thinking of making it for Tim."

"He'd just get in trouble with it," said Ronald, who sometimes displayed a surprising understanding of human nature.

"You're probably right," I said. "Maybe I should make an interdimensional camera instead."

"A what?" asked Ronald, wrinkling his hamstery brow.

"Something that lets you look in on nearby dimen-sions."

"What's a dimension?"

The question was difficult, not because I didn't know the answer but because I wasn't sure how to

explain it. I stalled for time by patting my Veeblax, which had come into the room shortly after Ronald. The little shape-shifter was trying to imitate Ronald, but in a lazy kind of way, which meant it ended up looking something like a two-foot-high cross between a hamster and a lizard.

"A dimension is another world," I said at last.

"You mean, like another planet?" asked Ronald eagerly.

"No, no — it's another world that occupies the same space that we do."

Ronald looked totally baffled.

I glanced around the lab table and found a stretchable cord. I looped one end around my toe, then pulled it tight.

"Watch," I said, plucking the cord.

It began to vibrate.

"That's neat," said Ronald. He is a very good audience, because almost everything is new and exciting to him. "But what does it have to do with other worlds?"

"The cord is vibrating, which means it's never in exactly the same place from instant to instant. If you could get something else to vibrate at exactly the same speed, but starting just a millisecond *after* this one, they could both occupy the same space without running into each other. That's what dimensions are like. There are thousands of them, all overlapping but each in its own vibrational plane so that it is a totally separate universe."

Ronald put his paws on the sides of his head. "It makes my brain hurt!"

I laughed. "Well, think about something else. I have to work now."

"I'll just read," said Ronald, taking one of his tiny books out of his pocket.

"You want to sit up here?" I asked.

Barvgis, the Fatherly One's personal assistant, had made some little armchairs for Ronald, and I kept one of them in the lab.

"That would be nice," said Ronald.

I took the chair out of the drawer where I kept it and set it on the lab table. Ronald climbed in, wiggled his butt a couple of times to get comfortable, then settled down to read.

Two or three hours later I had finished the camera — a tall, silvery box with tubes that pointed to a nearby screen that would display whatever dimension I tuned in.

Aliens, Underwear, and Monsters

Holding my breath, I turned on the camera and began dialing for dimensions. A moment later I let out a fart of excitement. "It's working!" I cried.

Ronald came trotting across the lab table.

"That's really weird," he said when he saw the bizarre shapes of the world revealed on the screen.

"Thank you," I replied.

Though Ronald's interest was nice, I wanted to show my machine to someone who would understand what skill it had taken for me to build it. My first choice would have been the Fatherly One, of course. But when I sent a message to his office, his secretary, Beezle Whompis, told me that he was tied up with business matters. I was not surprised. The Fatherly One has been extremely busy since we came to Earth—and even more busy since we discovered the planet's unexpected proximity to a Grand *Urpelli*.

An *urpelli* is a shortcut through space that makes interstellar travel possible. A Grand *Urpelli* links all the others into a galaxywide web, and the one near Earth is only the second ever discovered—which is why it's being called "Gurp Two." The thing is, it falls within the Earth franchise, which makes this poor, backward, underdeveloped world one of the most valuable properties in the galaxy — and the Fatherly One potentially the richest being ever known!

I can't think about that too much; if I do, I feel like Tim, who often says he thinks his head is going to explode. I never knew what he meant until all this started.

I decided to go look for McNally. I found him in the kitchen, talking to Barvgis, who is the roundest being I know and would rather be in the kitchen than anywhere else.

As I entered, Shhh-foop came sliding toward the table from the opposite direction. She was holding a steaming cup of black liquid in her tentacles.

"Here you go, Just McNally," she sang. "A new true brew for you."

She was starting to get better with her Earthling rhymes.

McNally looked terrified. Though he is a brave man with a warrior's heart, Shhh-foop's disastrous attempts at brewing this Earthly beverage have left him nervous about every new cup. However, he is too kind to refuse her when she offers some.

Aliens, Underwear, and Monsters

"Thanks, Shhh-foop," he said now, taking the mug from her outstretched tentacles.

She crooned a little song of nervousness as she watched him raise the cup to his lips. As he did, a small creature poked its head over the edge and spit some coffee at him.

"How did that squirmer get in there?" cried Barvgis. He reached over to pull the little creature out of the mug, then popped it into his mouth and chewed contentedly, ignoring its tiny screams.

McNally took a deep breath and set the coffee cup gently on the table. "Another time, Shhh-foop," he said softly. "Pleskit seems to need me right now."

"Alas, alas, failure and gloom rain always on my dreams of making the bean of caffeine sing to Just McNally's tongue," warbled Shhh-foop mournfully as she slid back to the counter.

McNally turned to me. "You showed up just in time, little buddy. What can I do for you?"

I smiled. "Glad to be of service," I whispered. "I wanted to know if you would like to take a look at my new science project."

"Be glad to," said McNally.

"I'll come, too," said Barvgis, lurching to his feet to join us.

I was very pleased.

"Had a good workout with Tim today," said McNally casually as we headed for the lab.

"That's nice," I said. I am still trying to analyze my emotional response to the fact that my bodyguard is giving these lessons to Tim, even though it had been my suggestion. I think the reason McNally mentioned it is that he would like me to join them for the lessons. However, Koo Muk Dwan is not something in which I am interested.

"Whoa, Pleskit!" said McNally when I had explained the interdimensional camera and dialed up a new dimension to display. "That is some weird stuff you got there!"

"I can tune in many other dimensions, too," I said proudly, making some adjustments.

McNally's eyes widened as I turned the knob. "Yikes!" he said in a low voice.

I turned to the screen, then jumped back in surprise.

CHAPTER 3

[TIM]
ALIEN VISITOR

Sitting on my dresser, reading one of my comic books, was a little orange-skinned alien — an alien I knew all too well.

"Beebo!" I cried. "What are *you* doing here?"

"Well, *that's* a nice greeting! Where is the exuberant expression of joy, the outpouring of delighted enthusiasm, the gleeful —"

"Glad to see you," I interrupted, though I wasn't entirely sure that I meant it.

"Better, but not overwhelming," said Beebo, giving me one of his wounded-puppy-dog faces. I had to fight down an emotion that made me want to fling myself to the floor and beg his forgiveness for making him feel bad.

That's one of the problems with Beebo. With his huge eyes and pointed ears, the little alien (he stands just under two feet tall) is so incredibly cute that it's almost impossible to resist him. The thing is, he is also an incredible amount of trouble — as I knew all too well from his last visit to Earth. His full name is Beebo Frimbat, and he claims to be a prince on the planet Roogbat — Prince of Mischief, to be more precise, a term that is well chosen.

I noticed that he had cleared a space on my desk by shoving aside some of my stacks of stuff — including three very valuable *Tarbox Moon Warriors* comic books and the remains of a peanut butter sandwich. (My mother claims my desk is a total mess. That may be true, but I pretty much had an idea what was in those stacks, and Beebo had just ruined my organizational system.)

Trying to stay calm, I said, "I wasn't expecting you, that's all. It's not as if Earth is on any of the common trade routes. It must have been a long way out of the way for you to come here." I looked at him suspiciously.

Aliens, Underwear, and Monsters

"Or did you sneak through Gurp Two? It's not supposed to be open for business yet, you know!"

Beebo just smiled. "There are things it is better not to know, Tim. Anyway, the reason I came is that I wanted to see you and Pleskit again." He paused and, looking a little embarrassed, added, "I also needed to retrieve my diary."

I began to relax a little. Beebo had left his diary behind the last time he was here, and I knew it was part of a school assignment he had. If he was just here for a short visit while he picked up the little book, it shouldn't mean much trouble.

"I also need to retrieve my body suit," he said.

"I thought you said you had no use for it," I replied, beginning to wonder if he wanted to see me and Pleskit at all. Not that I wouldn't be just as glad to have the body suit out of my closet. Beebo had worn it when he'd been pretending to be an Earth kid, and the thing was so realistic that it weirded me out at night, since it looked like a real (but lifeless) human being standing in my closet.

Beebo looked a little embarrassed. "I was informed by Sookutan Krimble that the body suit is very valuable, and that I should not have left it, even though it was not functioning properly."

"How is *Frek* Krimble?" I asked, using the proper term of respect for Beebo's mentor/relative. *Frek* Krimble is a tall, distinguished-looking being, who resembles Beebo only in that *yeeble* is orange. You would never guess the two of them were related. But on Roogbat it takes several kinds of beings to make a complete family unit.

A strange look flitted over Beebo's face when I asked about Sookutan Krimble. "My supervising relative is doing fine," he replied quickly. "*Yeeble* sends *yeeble*'s regards."

I would have asked more, but just then one of the books on my desk stood up and spread its arms. I laughed out loud. It was my Veeblax, which has been trying to learn new shapes lately. I had hatched the little guy from an *oog-slama* that had come from Pleskit's Veeblax.

The Veeblax made a happy yeeping sound and leaped down from the desk. It scurried across the room to where I was standing, then grew a couple of extra hands so it could climb my leg. When it was partway up my thigh, I reached down and lifted it onto my shoulder. It settled into its resting form, which is somewhat lizard-like, though with bigger eyes than any lizard ever had.

"I see your pet is growing," said Beebo. "You must be treating him well."

I felt a surge of pride. The Veeblax is the first pet Mom has ever allowed me to have, and I am trying hard to take good care of it. My pride was shoved aside by a surge of panic when I heard Beebo's next words.

"I figured this was a good time to come visit," he said, standing up and walking across my desk, "because I have a bit of a vacation. We had so much fun the last time that I thought it would be nice to stay for a few days."

Beebo does have the ability to make me laugh hysterically. Even so, his idea of fun is not always exactly the same as mine.

In fact, fun with Beebo is the kind of thing that can get a person in real trouble.

I decided I had better call Pleskit.

CHAPTER 4

[P L E S K I T]
SLOW MONSTERS

We were staring at monsters—strange mis-shapen creatures that stalked and crawled across a barren landscape made of twisting shapes that might have been rocks or might have been some weird plant growth. Evil-looking vapors swirled around the monsters' feet. Most, but not all, had two arms and two legs; I counted other numbers of each, ranging up to six. Some of the monsters were clearly traveling in packs. Most, though, seemed to be loners and snarled if they got too close to each other.

"Is there something wrong with the viewer?" asked McNally after a minute.

"I don't think so," I replied. "Why?"

"They're moving so slowly. It's kind of weird."

"I think that's just the way they are," said Barvgis. "I've read about this dimension. It's actually called 'the Monster Dimension' because the creatures in it are so horrible."

Two of the creatures had crossed paths and had started to fight. Though their movements were slow, they were powerful.

"Let's look at something more pleasant," said McNally uneasily.

I was about to change the viewer's setting when I heard a crackling behind us. I turned and saw, as I had expected, that the Fatherly One's secretary, Beezle Whompis, had manifested himself.

Beezle Whompis is an energy being and exists mostly in that state. It is difficult for him to take physical form; he only does it as a matter of courtesy when he needs to talk to us solid beings. When he does materialize, he is tall and lean, with huge dark eyes and hollow cheeks.

"Your Fatherly One wishes to see you, Pleskit," he said now.

Aliens, Underwear, and Monsters

I farted the tiny fart that is much like an Earthling's sigh. I had been having a good time with McNally and Barvgis and did not want it to end. On the other hand, I do not get to see the Fatherly One nearly as often as I would like, so I was not entirely distressed.

"I will be right there," I said.

Beezle Whompis nodded, then glanced at the screen. "Interesting," he said. "You've built an inter-dimensional camera. You didn't use the *gukstet* design, did you?"

"Actually, I did. Why?"

"The design has a flaw that makes it easy to alter the camera so it creates a full-dimensional gateway. Not that it really matters here, since it's unlikely anyone would tamper with it."

"A gateway?" asked McNally.

"It's an opening that would let someone enter the other dimension," said Beezle Whompis. "Fortunately, it's a one-way possibility. You certainly wouldn't want those things coming back this way! Of course, as an energy being, I couldn't cross through anyway. It would totally disrupt my field, and there's no telling how I would come out on the other side. Probably as nothing but a cloud of electrons. Well, I'd better get going. Things are incredibly busy these days. You'd better hurry, Pleskit. I don't think your Fatherly One wants to wait."

He nodded to McNally and Barvgis, then vanished.

"Better get going," said McNally.

I could tell by the tingle of energy in the air that Beezle Whompis was already at his desk by the time I reached the Fatherly One's office.

"Do you know what this is about?" I asked.

"I'm sure the ambassador will tell you soon enough," he said, without actually materializing.

I noticed the bag of energy snacks that my Hevi-Hevian friend Maktel had brought as a guesting gift on his ill-fated visit. It was sitting on Beezle Whompis's desk.

"Do you like those?" I asked.

Now Beezle Whompis did materialize. "I'm down to the last few," he said, staring at the bag wistfully. He reached into the bag and took out a glowing blue sphere. "They were some of the best I've ever had." He tossed the sphere into his mouth. A crackle of energy surrounded him. "Ah," he said in tones of deep satisfaction. "That was lovely."

"I'll be sure to tell Maktel how much you like them when I communicate with him," I said.

As we were talking, a short, birdlike female came out of the Fatherly One's office.

"Greetings, Pleskit," she said, waving her feathery brows at me.

"Greetings, *Wakkam* Akkim," I replied, tucking my hands into my armpits and making a slight bow. The *wakkam* is the Fatherly One's ethical adviser and spiritual massage-master, and I have great respect for her wisdom.

"Your Fatherly One is ready to see you," she said.

My parental unit was sitting in his command pod, which was floating slightly above my eye level. The pod's deeply padded chair is surrounded by a clear blue shell that curves over and around it, leaving a two-foot-wide opening in the front. As I entered the room, the pod slowly descended.

The Fatherly One stepped out and embraced me. "It is good to see you, my childling," he said.

Our "conference" was mostly about the state of the embassy's mission, and the number of outside threats we are facing now that the rest of the galaxy has realized the incredible value of the Earth trading franchise.

After we had discussed most of the problems my parental unit was facing, he said, "The final issue, and one that truly disturbs me, is the ongoing reports from Earthly newspapers that I am romantically involved with Ms. Buttsman."

"My Fatherly One is an interplanetary sex symbol," I said.

"This is not a joking matter, Pleskit," he replied. "It could have a very negative effect on our mission."

I tried not to laugh. Ms. Buttsman—"the Butt," as Tim calls her—is the Earthling assigned to the embassy by our host government to act as protocol adviser, and she is about as romantically appealing as the Fart of Doom.

"I apologize for making light of the situation," I said. But I was having a hard time holding in my smile, and a moment later the Fatherly One burst out laughing as well. Soon we were howling and belching with glee, slapping the table in our merriment. We only stopped when Ms. Buttsman herself came in to see if something was the matter.

"It's nothing!" gasped the Fatherly One. "Nothing at all!"

I could tell it was almost impossible for him to speak while he was looking at her.

When she left, we laughed again, and it reminded me of the old days, before the Fatherly One had become so important. I felt a little sad about that, and very happy that we were laughing like this now, and then sad again when he said, "I regret to tell you that I have to leave for another trip tomorrow, Pleskit."

My pleasure in the moment vanished. I could tell that the Fatherly One felt genuine guilt about the amount of time he spent away from me. However, I was beginning to be very distressed by his absences.

"Don't worry about it," I said, rather more sharply than I should have. "The staff will take good care of me!"

The Fatherly One reached out to me, but I turned and left the room, feeling unhappy with both him and myself. I went to my own room. But before I could dwell on the situation, my comm-device odored an alert, letting me know that I had an incoming call from Tim.

I turned it on and saw his face appear on the screen.

"Can you get over here?" he said, his voice low and urgent. "We've got company!"

"Who is it?"

Tim rolled his eyes. "I'd rather not say. I just think it would be a good idea if you could come over."

"I will have to see if McNally is available," I said.

I burped a request. The embassy locator system informed me that McNally had remained in the laboratory. I found him still staring in fascination at the monster dimension.

"I would like to go to Tim's," I said.

He glanced at his watch. "Getting kind of late for that, isn't it?"

"I agree. However, something has come up."

McNally groaned. "What now?"

"I do not know. But I think we should find out."

"All right," he said with a sigh. "Let's get going."

I turned off the interdimensional camera, and we headed for the base of the embassy.

"Bye!" called Ronald as we left the lab. "See you later!"

Aliens, Underwear, and Monsters

Ralph-the-Driver was in the garage — he always is — and we asked him to take us to Tim's apartment.

He nodded and got into the limousine. He didn't say anything. He never does. But as we settled into our seats, I saw him bend over and flip a small switch under the dashboard. I wondered what that was about. I would have asked Ralph, but since he had never said anything to me in all the months he had driven me, it felt strange to talk to him. I even thought it might offend him. So I figured I would just ask McNally about it later.

I would have, too, except that before the night was over, I had bigger things to think about.

CHAPTER 5

[TIM]
BEEBO BEGS

Within the first hour we were together, Beebo managed to make me totally forget what a pest he could be, mostly because he started telling me alien jokes. I only got half of them, but I think I liked it even better when I didn't understand them, because then he would explain what they were all about.

It's amazing how much you can learn about a place by trying to understand its jokes.

Beebo was just giving me the rundown on why his people find toe jam so screamingly funny when the doorbell rang.

"That's probably Pleskit and McNally," I said.

Aliens, Underwear, and Monsters

Beebo ran to the door as if they were long-lost friends.

He acted the same way an hour later when my mother showed up from work. Mom was tired and a little bit crabby — it had clearly been a tough day at the hospital — but when she saw Beebo, she got a big smile on her face. It got even bigger when she saw McNally. I'm starting to get the impression she kind of likes him. That's okay with me; I like him, too. The only problem is, I think he might like Ms. Weintraub, and I really don't like the idea of my mother and my teacher fighting over the same guy. It would make life entirely too complicated. But then, that's my feeling about romance in general, which is one reason I am in no hurry to get involved with it.

Unfortunately, there's another part of my brain, immune to common sense, that keeps thinking about Rafaella in ways I find very confusing. It is so annoying to have your mind out of control like that!

I made Mom a pot of tea, which always relaxes her a little. After she had had her feet up for a while, she asked if McNally and Pleskit would like to stay for dinner.

"I was hoping you'd ask," said McNally with a big smile. He likes Mom's cooking.

I think he gets too much alien food at the embassy.

Of course, the dinner invitation meant *I* got sent out to the grocery store to pick up a few extra things. Normally I wouldn't have minded, but I hated to leave when there were two aliens in the apartment. But Pleskit and Beebo couldn't come with me, and McNally couldn't come either, because even though our apartment is safe, he has a duty to stay close to Pleskit whenever they're out of the embassy.

When I got back with the bag of food, Mom and McNally were already working in the kitchen, and Beebo was helping — or, at least, trying to help — by floating stuff around with his telekinetic powers.

"I do not like this," said Pleskit in a low voice, when I went into the living room after unpacking the groceries.

"Don't like what?" I asked. "I think it's great having you all here."

"Beebo!" he said urgently. "He may be charming and funny, but you know the kind of trouble he can cause!"

I realized at once that Pleskit had a point. I had just gotten carried away with how much fun I was having.

Aliens, Underwear, and Monsters

"Well, how do we get rid of him?" I asked.

"I'm not sure. If we offend him, he might retaliate with some horrible joke. However, I'm sure he can't stay forever. We'll just have to be on our guard."

I would have enjoyed dinner more if we hadn't had that conversation, but I knew Pleskit was right—which was why I got even more nervous when Beebo said, "I would like to get my body suit working again."

"Why?" I asked.

"I would like to study the ways of Earthlings more fully. Also, it would be fun to visit your school as a student, rather than hiding in your backpack."

This was a reference to the way I had taken him to school on his last trip here.

"Do you have any idea what's wrong with the thing?" asked my mother, not realizing what an incredibly bad idea this was.

"It may just be what you Earthlings call 'out of gas,'" said Beebo. "An infusion of energy might be all it needs."

"Too bad you can't give it one of those energy snacks Beezle Whompis likes to munch on," said McNally. "Pass the salt, would you, Beebo?"

While Beebo was making the salt shaker float across the table, my mother said, "What do you mean, energy snacks? Are those like those high-calorie bars the athletes use?"

Pleskit laughed. "Beezle Whompis cannot eat solid food, Mrs. Tompkins. He is an energy being, and therefore consumes pure energy. Actually, he could feed himself quite well just by plugging into one of your wall sockets. But he prefers specialized forms of energy, such as the snacks that Maktel brought on his visit."

"Those might work!" said Beebo enthusiastically. "Do you suppose he would lend me some of them?"

"I don't know," said Pleskit. "He's running kind of low, and he really likes them."

"Oh, please see if he'll let me try one," said Beebo. He jumped down from his seat and ran around to Pleskit's chair. Dropping to his knees, he clutched his hands in front of him and cried, "Please, please, please, please, please."

Beebo's begging routine is something to see, since he pulls out every cute trick in the book when he does it. He is dangerously adorable. Imagine something three times cuter than a kitten, with the devious intel-

Aliens, Underwear, and Monsters

ligence of a politician, and you'll have a good sense of why Beebo can cause so much trouble. I was having a hard time not falling for his begging myself, and I could see my mother melting just watching him.

It took a while, but eventually Pleskit gave in. "I'll see what I can do," he said.

From such tiny seeds do great disasters grow.

CHAPTER 6

[PLESKIT]
ENERGY SNACKS

When McNally and I got into the limo to go back to the embassy for the energy snack, I paid close attention to Ralph-the-Driver. But I did not see him reach under the dashboard again. I decided I had been being overcautious when I found the gesture worrisome.

McNally waited until we were inside the embassy to discuss Beebo.

"I am not happy that he is back," he said as we stepped out of the tube that had lifted us from the underground parking garage into the embassy.

"Not happy that *who* is back?" asked a cold voice that caused me to jump in surprise.

Aliens, Underwear, and Monsters

It was the ever-unpleasant Ms. Buttsman, who had slipped quietly up behind us.

When neither McNally nor I answered her question right away, she said, "Can I assume you two have been over at that horrible Tompkins boy's apartment?"

"I cannot tell a lie," said McNally. "We did it. It's not against protocol to visit a friend, is it?"

"Not against the rules," said Ms. Buttsman coldly. "Just a violation of common sense. Pleskit should be cultivating friendships that will give him a better sense of our planet's cultural and intellectual resources. I hate to think of the impression of Earth he's getting at Tim's place."

"You're right," said McNally. "Exposing him to *real* human beings is probably a big mistake."

Ms. Buttsman curled her lip and stalked away.

"Makes me ashamed to be an Earthling," muttered McNally. "Come on, kid, let's go check on Beezle Whompis."

Beezle Whompis was in his office, talking with Eargon Fooz, a refugee from the planet Billa Kindikan who is staying in the embassy until she can return to her own people. Eargon Fooz has a body somewhat like the Earthling animal called a horse — except for the humanoid arms that grow from her shoulders. Her long, narrow face has four eyes and four ears, and is strangely beautiful.

I feel a deep bond with her, partly because we share the sorrow of being far from our home planets, partly because without her help my friends and I would surely have perished when we were stranded on her planet. Unfortunately, while helping us she was abducted to the forbidden city of Ilbar-Fakkam and cannot return to her people until a year has passed. I find this superstitious requirement extremely silly. But I have learned that there is no point in arguing with people's religious beliefs.

She seemed happy to see me. So did Beezle Whompis, though he became less so when I asked him if we could use one of his energy snacks.

"I only have three left," he said, in a somewhat more mournful voice than I am used to hearing from him.

"We might have a better chance of getting Beebo to wrap up his visit if we can get that suit working," I said.

"I agree," said McNally. "The little guy seemed

pretty nervous about the thing. I think he's in some kind of trouble for leaving it here."

Beezle Whompis made a staticky noise that I knew to be his equivalent of a sigh. "Then you had better take one," he said. "Beebo is not someone we want around any longer than necessary."

After removing the ball of energy from its bag, Beezle Whompis wrapped it carefully in something made of the same protective material.

"Be careful," he said. "It's very powerful."

"You got it!" cried Beebo in delight when we returned to the apartment an hour later. "Oh, this is wonderful! Come on, let's go get the body suit."

"Is there a path?" asked McNally.

The reason he asked this question is that making a trip across Tim's room is a little like going on an archae-ological dig. There's a lot of debris in the way, and you never know what you'll find underneath it.

"One path coming up,"' said Tim's mother quickly, grabbing Tim by the arm. I could tell she was embar-rassed to have McNally see Tim's room, which truly is a galaxy-class *foojstad*.

"We have a deal," she said over her shoulder as they started down the hall. "As long as he keeps his mess out of the rest of the apartment, I don't get in his face about what's in his room."

Fifteen minutes later they called out for us to join them. A strip of visible floor space about a foot wide led from his door across to the closet. Scattered on either side of it was an astonishing jumble of laundry, books, comic books, drawings, toys, games, crumpled papers, food, things that looked like food, and things too mystifying to guess at.

"Have you ever lost anyone in here?" asked Beebo, who was standing in the doorway.

"I'd rate that a minus one," growled Tim, referring to Beebo's habit of grading people's jokes.

I've noticed that my friend is never amused when people comment on the state of his room.

McNally retrieved the body suit, which looked eerily like a perfectly formed but totally lifeless human boy. He stood it with its back to the dining room table. The reason he did this was that the way in and out of it was through a door that opens in the back. You can't see the door when it's closed; the lines blend perfectly so that the suit's back looks like unbroken flesh. But Beebo knew where the top of the door was, and quickly pried it open. It was about eight inches wide and a foot high, and it was hinged at the bottom. When he pulled it down, it formed a ramp leading from the table into the interior of the body suit.

I handed him the energy snack.

He went up the ramp and climbed into the suit.

"Wish me luck," he said, poking his head out.

"Good luck," we all said.

He pulled up the ramp. It closed against the back of the body suit, sealing itself so that it once again disappeared.

We waited.

Nothing happened.

"Do you suppose he's okay?" asked Mrs. Tompkins after several minutes had gone by. "He's not trapped, is he?"

"Beebo!" I called. "Are you all right in there?"

Suddenly the suit's eyes blinked open.

"Skrreeeeba-kottzle!" it shrieked, looking for all the world like a human kid who had just gone stark raving mad.

Then the trouble really began.

CHAPTER 7

[TIM]
OUT OF CONTROL

I jumped back as the body suit, or Beebo, or whatever, began waving its arms and cackling like a maniac.

It began to hop around the room. The hops took it higher and higher, until it was actually crashing against the ceiling.

"Someone stop it!" cried my mother.

That was easier said than done. Suddenly the suit stopped hopping and began running in circles. Then it leaped onto the dining room table and began shaking so hard, it looked as if it were trying to break its arms and legs loose. And all this time it was laughing—a strange, horrible laugh that was even scarier than its weird actions.

"Hee-yuh Fwah!" cried McNally suddenly, moving into the Koo Muk Dwan position that I recognized as "the Chop of Suey." Hands flying, feet flashing, larynx quavering, he flung himself against Beebo's body suit. It was a strange battle, because the body suit didn't actually fight so much as thrash around wildly. You couldn't anticipate its moves, but it wasn't really trying to hurt McNally, either.

"Hellguhlllp meeeee!" it cried, and for the first time the sounds coming out of its mouth were something like words. They were so filled with fear, it almost broke my heart to hear them.

"Do something, McNally!" cried my mother.

"He's trying!" I said, pushing her back toward the kitchen so she wouldn't get hurt if the two of them came rolling in our direction.

McNally and Beebo were in the living room now, where the suit resumed hopping. Finally McNally managed to seize the body suit around the waist. They crashed to the floor. The suit thrashed wildly, its arms and legs jerking and twitching. McNally grabbed first one arm and then the other. He held them tight as the

suit slowly stopped twitching, almost like a little kid calming down from a tantrum.

Finally it blinked twice, then said in a perfectly normal voice, "Thank you, McNally. That energy snack was obviously more potent than I expected."

"I'm surprised Beezle Whompis doesn't explode when he eats them," said Pleskit in awe.

"Are you all right?" asked my mother.

"You talking to me or Beebo?" growled McNally.

"Both of you."

"I don't know about the kid, but I'm pretty banged up," said McNally.

"I am shaken, but not stirred," said Beebo

"Yeah, but are you in control?" asked McNally, who was still holding Beebo.

"I believe so. If you will let go of one arm, I will see if I can move it properly."

Looking nervous, McNally did as Beebo asked. The body suit lifted its arm, twisted it, bent it at the elbow, lowered it again.

"The crisis seems to have passed," said Beebo.

McNally grunted and let go of him. They both got to their feet. We followed Beebo back to the dining room, where he backed up to the table, lowered the door, and climbed out of the body suit. As he was doing this, McNally stretched and groaned. "I think I'm going to need the Heal-a-tron tonight," he said.

"We'll have to see if we can calibrate it for Earthlings," said Pleskit.

"Too bad you don't have a Heal-a-tron for rooms," said Mom, sounding mournful.

I looked around.

Both the living room and the dining room looked a lot like my bedroom.

"The boys will get right on it, ma'am," said McNally, collapsing with a groan into one of the easy chairs.

I sighed and started cleaning—which was when I discovered what a disaster Beebo's rampage had truly been.

"My father's Tarbox!" I cried. *"You broke my father's Tarbox!"* It was all I could do to keep from bursting into tears. "You are such a little menace!" I shouted.

Beebo *did* burst into tears. "That's no way to talk to a friend!"

"You're no friend of mine!" I snapped, staring in horror at the two halves of the beautiful little ship.

Beebo gasped and ran out of the room. None of

us went after him immediately, but then we heard the outside door. I realized he must have used his tele-kinetic powers to open it.

"Wait!" cried my mother. "Beebo, wait!"

The door slammed shut.

"Oh, no!" cried Mom. "Go after him, McNally!"

McNally sighed and heaved himself to his feet. He shot me a look, then ran out of the room. As we heard him leave the apartment, my mother turned on me.

"Now look what you've done," she said.

"What *I've* done?" I cried angrily. I held up the bro-ken ship. "What about *this*?"

Before she could answer, McNally was back in the room. "He's gone already," he said. "Come on, we'll all have to look for him. Pleskit, you stick with me."

Pleskit sighed but didn't argue. Sometimes I feel sorry for him. It must be rough never being able to get off on his own.

We hurried out of the apartment. We searched the building from the top floor to the bottom, without finding a sign of Beebo.

"Outside," said McNally. "Mrs. T, you take the back of the building. Tim, you check out front. Pleskit and

I will look in the woods. Stay close to me," he added sternly, speaking to Pleskit.

We searched for nearly an hour, calling Beebo's name and shouting for him to come back.

He didn't answer, and we couldn't find the slightest sign of him.

Finally we had to give up. "I've got to get Pleskit back to the embassy, or Buttsman will have my head for a hat rack," said McNally.

"But poor little Beebo . . . ," said my mother mournfully.

I wanted to puke. "Beebo crosses interstellar space on his own, Mom. He can take care of himself."

She just glared at me.

I turned to Pleskit. "Let's get to school early tomorrow. Maybe he'll show up there."

Pleskit nodded, and McNally groaned. "So much for that good night's sleep," he said.

I didn't get much sleep myself that night. I was heartbroken about the ruined Tarbox. At the same time I was wracked with guilt over the harsh words I had spoken to Beebo. Despite my assurances to Mom that he would be fine, I couldn't help picturing him lost, lonely, afraid. . . .

CHAPTER 8

[TIM]
FLAPPING IN THE BREEZE

I got up early, just as Pleskit and I had planned. I could tell Mom approved by the fact that she got up and cooked me breakfast, something she doesn't usually do these days.

"Good luck," she said. "I hope you find him."

If I had known what I was in for, I would have said, "I hope I don't!"

But that came later. I hopped onto my bike and headed for school. The embassy limousine rolled in at about the same time I did. Pleskit and McNally climbed out. As they did, Pleskit pointed up and said, "What's that?"

I looked up and staggered in horror.

At the top of the school flagpole, rippling in the spring breeze, was a pair of red-and-white-striped boxer shorts.

What made this particularly unfortunate was the fact that they were mine.

"This may be the end of my life," I groaned.

Pleskit looked at me in surprise. "Why are you so distressed? It's only an undergarment."

"Do you have any idea of the potential for embarrassment that's flapping up there right now?" I cried.

"*I* do!" shouted a small voice from above us.

I looked up again and saw Beebo poking his little orange face over the waistband of my boxers and smirking down at us. "You should have treated me better!" he yelled.

"Beebo, you maniac!" I cried in exasperation. "Get down from there!"

"I don't think I will," he said happily. "I like it up here. The view is fine. And your amusing undergarment offers a nice seat!"

He stuck his feet through the leg holes—he was so short, they barely came through—and started to swing back and forth.

Aliens, Underwear, and Monsters

"How did you get those, anyway?" I demanded.

"I have my little ways," he said merrily.

By this time some of the other kids were starting to gather around us, laughing and pointing. When he noticed them coming, Beebo pulled his feet in and ducked his head so the kids wouldn't see him.

"Whose underwear are they?" asked Chris Mellblom, who sounded disgustingly amused.

"I don't know," said Michael Wu. "I'm just glad they're not mine!"

I stifled a groan. Maybe if I didn't say anything, didn't let on that the boxers were mine, I might be able to avoid total humiliation.

The idea seemed to be working . . . until Jordan showed up. "Hey, Tim!" he hooted. "What's your underwear doing flying from the flagpole? Do you really want everyone to salute your shorts?"

"Good one, Jordan," snorted Brad Kent, who is sort of Jordan's official suck-up and lapdog.

"How do you know they're mine?" I asked, trying to head things off. "You been studying my underwear, Jordan? I didn't know you cared!"

"Ooooh!" said everyone, which let me know I'd scored.

Jordan's eyes widened; clearly he saw my comment as a challenge. "I saw them in gym class once," he snapped. "I haven't been able to forget, since they were the most uncool things I ever saw in my life. I was afraid it might be catching."

This got another "Ooooh," though not as strong as the one I had received, which made me feel good. I was trying to come up with another solid comeback when I noticed Rafaella standing nearby. She was starting to blush.

The sight of her completely discombobulated me, and I started to blush myself. Jordan stood there, staring at me, waiting for me to come up with a zinger. I probably looked like a goldfish, my mouth opening and closing but no words coming out.

My misery was ended, sort of, by a deep voice from behind me bellowing, "All right, all right! That's about enough of this nonsense. Everyone, into the building. *Now!*"

It was Principal Grand.

I will not repeat the many supposedly hilarious comments that were made to me as we went to our classrooms. I will only say that I went to my desk thinking that maybe those times when I had been shrunk down to only a few inches high hadn't been so bad after all. I would have been perfectly willing to shrink out of sight right then.

I glanced through the window and saw Mr. Brimslow, the custodian, lowering my shorts.

Beebo seemed to have disappeared. At least, he was not in the boxers when Mr. Brimslow took them off the flagpole chain.

A few minutes later we heard a knock at the classroom door. When Ms. Weintraub opened it, I saw Mr. Brimslow standing there with my boxers in his hand.

"I understand these belong to someone in here," he said, holding my boxers up good and high so everyone could see.

"Oh, Tim!" cried Jordan in a high voice. "Your laundry's here!"

I trudged to the front of the room to collect the wretched underwear. People were howling with laughter. Brad Kent was slapping his desk and gasping for breath. Even Pleskit and Ms. Weintraub were smiling, the traitors.

Bruce Coville

Blushing as red as the stripes on my boxers, I crammed them into my backpack.

I couldn't wait to get my hands on that little beast, Beebo.

I had no idea that someone else had already gotten to him.

CHAPTER 9

[BEEBO]
ROOFTOP MEETING

All right, maybe I went too far. It happens now and then. But how was I to know that Earthlings are so ridiculously uncomfortable with their bodies and the undergarments that cover them? I mean, when I snitched the underwear, I knew it could be used to embarrass Tim. But I felt he had a little embarrassment coming. I certainly hadn't expected him to act as if it would be fatal.

I must say that I had found sitting in his shorts at the top of the flagpole quite pleasant. It was a sweet, cool morning, and I could see a long way across Tim's city, which is a nice little place, even if it is very primitive.

Suddenly I noticed someone coming toward the flagpole, almost certainly with the intent of pulling down my perch.

Fortunately, I was wearing my flying belt.

(Only an idiot would put himself in a situation like that without a flying belt, and whatever else I may be, I am not an idiot. At least, I didn't think I was. However, as you will see, I was about to make a mistake that was both hideous and foolish.)

Anyway, I jetted over to the school roof. It was a broad, flat space surrounded by a little wall about as high as my knees.

To my surprise, I noticed many colorful spheres scattered across the roof's surface. At first, I could not imagine their purpose. Were they here for some sort of experiment? Were they gathering solar energy? Then, about an hour after I had been there, another sphere came flying over the edge of the roof.

"You moron!" I heard someone shout from down below. "Now we'll never get our ball back!"

I laughed out loud. The balls were just balls. It had never occurred to me that they might be up there by accident. I had forgotten that the Earth kids couldn't just fly up to get them.

I was trying to decide whether to startle the kids by throwing the ball back to them when I heard a voice behind me say, "Put up your hands. Now!"

I spun around and saw a small, furry being in an orange uniform. She didn't stand much taller than my knee, but she was carrying a ray gun, and she was pointing it right at me.

"Hands up," she said again.

"Don't shoot!" I cried, doing as she ordered. "I am innocent!"

Actually, this was not entirely true. I am far from innocent, and have done many very naughty things in my short life. However, I was taught early on that it is always wise to try to *appear* innocent in a situation such as this.

"Who are you?" snarled the creature.

"My name is Beebo," I said. "Beebo Frimbat. And who are you?"

"They call me Doris . . . Doris the Delightful."

The furry creature did not strike me as being

particularly delightful, but I decided not to argue the point. It is never good to argue with someone holding a ray gun.

Doris circled me, studying me from all sides.

"Where are you from?" she demanded at last.

"The planet Roogbat."

"What are you doing here on Earth?"

"I came to visit friends," I said, not wanting to be too specific.

Aliens, Underwear, and Monsters

"I assume you mean Pleskit and his Fatherly One?" she said, sounding a trifle smug.

"That is correct." I was a little uncomfortable that she had figured this out so easily, until I realized it wasn't surprising, since Ambassador Meenom's group are the only off-worlders who are supposed to be on Earth anyway.

Doris stared at me for a moment. I had a feeling she was judging me. Then, suddenly, as if she had made a decision, she said, "How good a friend is Pleskit?"

"Good enough," I replied, not sure how much of a friend he actually considered *me* at the moment.

"Sit down," she said.

I sat. After all, she had the ray gun.

"All right, listen carefully," she said, squatting in front of me. "I have some serious information to give you." She paused, then said, "Do you know why I'm here?"

I wiggled my middle antenna, the sign of questioning, and asked, "Should I?"

"No! I'm supposed to be a secret. I work for a group that is looking out for Pleskit. I live in the walls of the school and keep an eye on him. However, I have learned that he is in great danger."

"From what?" I asked, feeling the tickle in my feet that always comes with a hint of adventure.

Doris glanced from side to side, then leaned closer and said, "There is a traitor in the embassy. Someone close to Pleskit wants to harm him."

"Who?" I asked.

"Do you know his bodyguard, McNally?"

"Of course."

Doris was silent for a long moment. The spring sun beat down, warming the dark surface of the roof. From below we could hear the shouts of the kids playing.

"Listen carefully," said Doris. "McNally has been brainwashed by evil aliens who want to sabotage Meenom's mission and kidnap Pleskit. McNally is just waiting for the right moment to strike. Pleskit will not believe you if you tell him this, for he is very loyal to McNally. This is not surprising; when you put your life in someone's hands, you must give that person your complete trust as well. But it makes it much harder to protect Pleskit from McNally. If you care for Pleskit at all, you *must* look for a way to get McNally out of the picture! Otherwise, Pleskit will remain in great danger!"

Aliens, Underwear, and Monsters

I felt a thrill in my knees. Perhaps this was my chance to make things up with Pleskit and Tim. If I saved Pleskit from his evil bodyguard, they would have to think highly of me, wouldn't they?

Then I realized this wasn't just about me, about trying to make myself look good in their eyes again.

I had a *duty* to save Pleskit from the evil McNally.

Somehow, I had to get rid of that menace!

CHAPTER 10

[PLESKIT]
TREACHERY

The afternoon of the underwear-on-the-flagpole incident I was very nervous. The reason was simple: before all this happened, I had invited Tim to come over that evening to see my science project.

I had also invited Rafaella.

And, at *Wakkam* Akkim's suggestion, I had invited Jordan.

The *wakkam's* explanation for this was typical of her. "Now that Tim and Jordan have survived a shared danger, the walls between them will be less solid," she had said. "This is a good time to draw them closer, and perhaps end their mutual enmity."

Aliens, Underwear, and Monsters

Wakkam Akkim seemed to think this was a good thing. She was ignoring the fact that Jordan had also been *my* enemy. Or maybe she wasn't. With *Wakkam* Akkim it can be hard to tell.

It had also been hard to tell Tim that Jordan would be coming over—especially after the underwear teasing. I had tried, more than once, but I had never actually managed to bring myself to say it. So he still didn't know. Which was why I was so nervous about what was going to happen when they all showed up.

I was sitting in the embassy kitchen, eating *febril gnurxis* and trying to explain all this to McNally, when the speaker system burped a high-priority request from the guardhouse where outsiders stop to seek permission to enter the embassy.

"I wonder if that's Jordan?" said McNally, who didn't seem all that happy about my having invited the classmate he generally refers to as "that puffed-up little rich boy."

"It's too early," I said. "Besides, I've already cleared him for admission. The guard wouldn't send a high-priority signal for him."

The mystery was solved a moment later when

Barvgis waddled into the kitchen and said, "Your friend Beebo is here. I gave permission for him to enter. He'll be up in a moment."

Ms. Buttsman had come striding in right behind him. "Really, Pleskit," she said, her eyes blazing. "As Earth's representative in the embassy, I must be warned if we are going to have interplanetary visitors. There are diplomatic protocols to be considered. There are contacts to make. There are —"

"I didn't know he was coming," I said.

Ms. Buttsman looked startled, and her mouth tightened. "Well, then, we'll have to speak to *him* about that, won't we? After all, there are protocols that *he* should have considered. There are —"

Just then Beebo came walking into the room. His big eyes looking both humble and hopeful, he flung himself at my feet and cried, "Please, please, please, please, please forgive me for my foolish action this morning!"

Ms. Buttsman stared at this in astonishment. "Is this your visitor?" she asked.

"Yes. Ms. Buttsman, allow me to present Beebo Frimbat, Prince of Roogbat," I said, giving him a formal introduction.

Aliens, Underwear, and Monsters

I was astonished when Ms. Buttsman smiled — the first smile I had seen from her that wasn't actually scary — and said, "Well, aren't you just the cutest thing!"

Beebo's secret weapon of being irresistibly adorable had worked again!

Soon we were all sitting at the table — even Ms. Buttsman, something that almost never happens.

"I am sorry about what I did this morning," Beebo said to me.

"I am not the one you need to apologize to," I replied.

"Do you think Tim is very angry with me?" asked Beebo, doing his big-eyed trick.

Ms. Buttsman patted his hand. "How could anyone stay angry with *you*?" she asked tenderly.

"Believe me," I said. "It's possible. However, in Tim's case, I would say the correct term is probably 'very, very, *very* angry.'"

Beebo sighed. "It is so easy to offend Earthlings."

"It's easy to offend people from any planet if you are not aware of their customs and quirks," said Ms. Buttsman sympathetically.

"Would it be all right if I stayed here tonight?" asked Beebo. "I have to go back to Roogbat soon, but I don't want to leave until I have made peace with Tim, and I do not think it is the proper time to return to his house."

"Of course," said Ms. Buttsman, before I could say anything about the fact that I had already invited Tim, Rafaella, and Jordan to come over later that evening to see my interdimensional camera.

Actually, it didn't make any difference. Even if I had wanted to boot Beebo out—which part of me did—the laws of hospitality have precedence over the rules of friendship.

"Tim will be coming over later," I warned him.

"For what reason?" asked Ms. Buttsman, sounding as if I had just announced I was planning to commit a major crime.

"I want to show him my new science project," I said somewhat sharply. "Rafaella and Jordan are coming too. It has already been approved."

Ms. Buttsman scowled, but Beebo looked interested. "I love science projects!" he said enthusiastically. "What have you made?"

"An interdimensional camera," I said, smiling proudly.

Aliens, Underwear, and Monsters

Suddenly he seemed even more interested. *Too* interested, I realized later.

"I made one of those once," he said. "Can I see it?"

"Sure," I replied, letting my eagerness to show off my work shove aside my annoyance with him. "Come on."

"It's a nice job," said Beebo when I took him to the lab where the camera was located. "*Gukstet* design, right? Mind if I stay here and scan dimensions for a while?"

I should have known he was up to something, but all I thought of at the moment was that it would keep him out of the way while Tim and the others were coming in.

So I told him it was fine.

How could I have guessed the depth of treachery lurking in that tiny orange breast?

CHAPTER 11

[TIM]
THE GANG'S ALL HERE— ALMOST

Pleskit didn't tell me he had invited Jordan to come over to the embassy, so I was startled and not entirely happy when he showed up. But I didn't say anything; I was willing to hold off until he started in on me. After he managed to go a full five minutes without saying anything rotten—which I think was an all-time record—I began to wonder if someone had convinced him he should act like a human being while he was at the embassy.

Or maybe Pleskit used some secret alien device to alter his personality and get him to behave decently. Who knows?

Aliens, Underwear, and Monsters

As for Jordan, he seemed really startled to meet Beebo. This surprised me, until I realized that even though the last time Beebo was here he had used his telekinetic powers to annoy Jordan, we had never told Jordan what was really happening.

I spent the first half hour trying to stay as far away from Jordan as I could without getting too close to Beebo. I found this confusing. I am basically a nice person and do not like to fight with people. So how did I end up with two enemies in the same room?

The person I did want to stand close to was Rafaella, but I was afraid that if I did, Jordan would have one more thing to tease me about.

"Some snacks, my little *keekle-boongers*?" sang Shhh-foop, sliding over to us. With her tentacles she was carrying a tray covered with glowing yellow blobs. "These are *kloopenzoofers*," she sang proudly. "I made them just for you."

"Thanks," said Rafaella, sounding a bit nervous as she took one of the blobs off the tray.

The *kloopenzoofers* tasted pretty good, but made weird squeaking sounds when you bit down on them. When everyone had had a couple, Pleskit suggested

we go to the lab for the demonstration of his interdimensional camera. I hoisted my backpack and followed the group, still uncertain how I felt about
Jordan having been invited into the embassy, and half
thinking I might just leave.

When we got to the lab, we found Ronald the mutant
hamster sitting in a tiny easy chair and reading a book.

"Tim!" he cried, leaping to his feet. "Rafaella!
Jordan! I am so pleased to see all of you!"

"Ohmigod," said Rafaella, who has this major thing
about hamsters. "You look so cute in that outfit,
Ronald!"

"Please," said Ronald, turning his head away and
acting shy. "You embarrass me."

"So what's this big invention, Pleskit?" asked Jordan.

As Pleskit was explaining the interdimensional
camera, McNally came strolling in.

"Pretty cool, huh?" he said, gesturing to the monitor. "Did you show 'em the monster dimension yet,
Pleskit?"

"Not yet," said Pleskit uneasily. "I wasn't sure I
should. It's awfully scary."

Aliens, Underwear, and Monsters

"Of course we want to see it!" said Jordan eagerly. "I love monsters!"

I started to say that this was probably because seeing monsters would be like a family reunion for him, but I bit my tongue in time. Jordan hadn't said anything rotten to me yet, and I didn't want to be the one to start things.

Rafaella seconded the motion. "I love monsters, too," she said.

"You do?" I asked in surprise.

She sighed. "I told you, Tim—there's a lot about me that you don't know. My parents let me have a room in the cellar that I use just for my collection of monster stuff."

I felt a weird fluttering in my chest. I didn't know it was possible for a girl to be this cool.

"All right," said Pleskit, still sounding a little uneasy. "I'll show you."

He dialed up the monster dimension.

We all gasped in a satisfactory manner, then watched in fascinated horror as the monsters dragged their way across the mist-covered landscape.

"How come they're so slow?" asked Rafaella.

"I don't know why, exactly," said Pleskit. "It's just something about that dimension. It's a pretty strange place."

"I'm going back to my book," said Ronald, climbing into his chair. "Beebo already spent a lot of time looking at that dimension today. I'm tired of it."

Beebo looked a little nervous, then smiled quickly and said, "Actually, I made a slight adjustment to the machine, because I knew how fascinated McNally was by the monsters."

Aliens, Underwear, and Monsters

"What did you do?" asked Pleskit, sounding a little angry.

That pleased me, since I was glad to have someone else upset with the little trickster.

"It's better if I just show you," said Beebo. "I think you'll like it, but it takes a little getting used to. We should let McNally see first, since he's so interested in this place. Stand here, McNally, to get the best view."

McNally looked a little puzzled. But then he shrugged and stood where Beebo asked. Maybe he should have been suspicious, but I think that since we were in the embassy, he figured he was safe.

"All right, just wait a second," said Beebo. He went to the control panel and pushed a button.

"What's that?" asked Pleskit. "I didn't put that button in when I —"

His words were cut off by a sizzling sound that made me clamp my hands over my ears. Suddenly a blaze of blinding green light filled the room.

I closed my eyes to shut out the light.

When I opened them again, McNally had vanished.

CHAPTER 12

[PLESKIT]
THE DIMENSIONAL DOOR

An oval of green light remained floating in the air where McNally had been standing. I noticed now what I should have seen before: two small devices mounted in the ceiling above, and two more below. The ones in the floor were very small, really just reflecting lenses, and easy to miss until you were looking for them.

"Beebo, what have you done?" I cried in horror. "And where is McNally?"

Before Beebo could answer, Tim shouted, "There he is! There, on the screen!"

"Holy crap!" said Jordan. "Look at that!"

Aliens, Underwear, and Monsters

I turned to the monitor and nearly went into *kleptra*. McNally had been transported into the monster dimension! He appeared baffled, dazed, terrified — all perfectly reasonable, under the circumstances. He was trying to walk, but it looked as if the ground was clinging to his shoes. He staggered a few feet, then turned. I could tell he was shouting, but we couldn't hear him.

He turned and walked on.

"This way!" I shouted. "McNally, this way!" But that was stupid of me, because I knew he couldn't hear me.

We all turned on Beebo. I really believe the little pest thought his life was in danger at that moment. Maybe it was. I, for one, was nearly insane with fury, something I had never felt before. It was a powerful and terrifying emotion.

"I did it for you, Pleskit!" cried Beebo, putting up his hands to ward us off. "I did it for you!"

"What are you talking about?" I cried. "What, exactly, did you do?"

He looked around wildly, as if trying to find an escape route, then said, "I fixed your camera so it would open a gateway into another dimension."

I couldn't believe what I was hearing. "Why would you do a thing like that?"

"So I could get McNally away from you."

He was down on his knees now, clutching his hands in front of him. But for once his cuteness was of no use. This time he had gone too far.

"You're working for Pleskit's enemies, aren't you?" cried Tim furiously. He seemed to take some grim pleasure in this idea. "You rotten little traitor!"

"That's not true!" cried Beebo. He stood up again, then threw back his shoulders and looked at us proudly. "I told you, I did it for Pleskit. You don't know it, but McNally is an evil force who wants to do Pleskit terrible harm."

"What in the world makes you think that?" I asked in astonishment.

"I learned it from a secret friend of yours. That's the reason I came back to the embassy this afternoon, even though I knew you were angry at me. I came to protect you."

"What secret friend?" I demanded.

"Her name is Doris. She lives in the walls of the school and watches over you."

Aliens, Underwear, and Monsters

"You idiot!" cried Ronald, leaping to his tiny feet. "Doris is evil. I should know — I used to live in the same cage with her. She wants to *destroy* Tim and Pleskit."

"That can't be true," said Beebo. He looked terrified, and a little sick. "She told me . . . she told me . . ."

"Whatever she told you was a lie," said Jordan angrily. "I've met Doris too. Believe me, she —"

His words were cut off by a scream from Rafaella. "Look! *Look!*"

We all turned back toward the monitor.

Three snorting, drooling monsters were lurching toward my beloved bodyguard. Though they were all behind him, each was coming from a slightly different direction. They were huge, with broad, knobby shoulders and arms so long that their knuckles dragged on the ground. One was greenish-brown and had a pointy head. One, bright red and slightly shorter, had a long flopping nose and enormous ears. The third, which was some weird color that made my eyes hurt, had a wide, gaping mouth filled with horrible fangs.

The worst thing was that McNally, who looked stunned, was facing away from them and was clearly unaware of their approach.

"McNally, watch out!" cried Tim.

McNally didn't respond, of course; he couldn't hear anything we said.

"Isn't there any way we can talk to him?" asked Rafaella urgently.

"The camera wasn't designed for that," I told her. "It was just meant to show the other world — not *send* people there," I added, shooting a vicious glance at Beebo.

He groaned and put his head between his hands. "I'm bad!" he cried, tugging on his antennae. "Oh, I am so bad!"

I turned back to the viewscreen.

The monsters were lurching closer to McNally. He had heard them at last. But when he tried to run, he couldn't pull his feet from the ground. He had been sinking into it, and now it was up to his ankles. He reached down and grabbed his knee, trying to wrench his foot free of the clinging, wobbling surface.

The three monsters continued toward him, their movements slow but steady.

CHAPTER 13

[TIM]
RONALD TAKES THE PLUNGE

"We've got to do something!" I shouted. "We can't let those things get McNally!"

"Call one of the adults, Pleskit," said Rafaella urgently.

"Who?" asked Pleskit. His *sphen-gnut-ksher* was sparking with anxiety. "The Fatherly One and Ms. Buttsman left for China. Beezle Whompis might give us some advice, but his nature as an energy being makes it impossible for him to cross between dimensions. The Grandfa—"

"Stop fussing and just put out an all-points alarm!" I shouted.

I glanced around. Beebo was sitting in the corner,

wringing his hands and looking guilty and terrified.

Good! I thought savagely. *That's just how you should feel.*

Pleskit ran to the wall and burped a message into the embassy's comm system. Soon we heard a whooping noise. A mellow voice began announcing, "There is an emergency in the lab. I repeat: there is an emergency in the lab."

Beezle Whompis crackled into sight almost instantly. His arrival made Jordan jump in a way that would have amused me if I hadn't been so worried about McNally. Barvgis came lumbering in a few moments later, his slimy flesh wobbling from his running. At about the same time, the Grandfatherly One's voice shouted over the comm system, "What the heck is going on in there?"

"We'll tell you later!" shouted Pleskit.

"Not later, sprout. I want to know now!"

"We don't have time to talk, sir!" I shouted. "McNally is trapped in another dimension with slow monsters creeping up on him, and we have to figure out a way to save him."

"Spoobergort!" cried the Grandfatherly One.

Pleskit looked shocked.

"Barvgis and I are here, sir," said Beezle Whompis. "We will do what we can."

Aliens, Underwear, and Monsters

The energy being turned to the rest of us and said calmly, "Please tell me exactly what happened."

Beebo groaned as we recounted the story. Barvgis looked more and more worried. I kept watching the screen. McNally was still struggling to free himself from the clinging muck. I wondered if he even knew that we could see him. He probably thought there was no chance of help at all. I tried to imagine what it must be like for him, but the feeling was so terrifying that I had to stop.

Barvgis turned to Beebo. "Was the gate you made a one-way or a two-way?"

"One-way," said Beebo miserably.

"You mean there's no way for McNally to get back from there?" asked Rafaella in horror.

"Not unless we create one," said Barvgis. "I can prepare a device that will open a two-way gate. Unfortunately, with one gate already opened here, the only way the second gate could be opened right now is from the other side. So we'd have to get it through to McNally for him to use it."

"Which makes it pointless," said Beezle Whompis.

"Why?" asked Rafaella.

"Because McNally's passage through the first gate used up so much energy that the remaining opening is now too small to let any of us through."

I started to suggest that we just toss the device through what was left of the gate, but immediately realized that would be pointless. McNally wouldn't be able to get to the device . . . and even if he could, we wouldn't be able to tell him how to use it, since he couldn't hear us.

"I can take it through," said Ronald.

We turned and looked at the little hamsteroid in astonishment.

"Someone has to do it," he said. "And I'm the only one who can fit."

"I don't know if you'll be able to carry the device," said Barvgis.

"Let me try," said Ronald.

"All right, we'll make it as small as we can. Pleskit, come on over here and give me a hand. Your fingers are more supple than mine."

"How long is this going to take?" I asked, not moving my eyes from the screen, where I could see the monsters making their slow way toward McNally.

Aliens, Underwear, and Monsters

"We can have it ready in about fifteen minutes," said Barvgis.

"Fifteen minutes!" cried Rafaella. "McNally might be gone by then!"

By "gone" she meant "dead," of course.

I was glad she didn't say the word out loud.

"We'll work as fast as we can," said Barvgis grimly.

Barvgis and Pleskit were a little faster than they'd predicted. They had the device ready in thirteen minutes and forty-two seconds. I know because I timed them. I think it was the longest thirteen minutes and forty-two seconds of my life. I paced the lab, feeling totally helpless and worthless. I couldn't stand to look at the monitor and couldn't stand to turn away from it.

The monsters were horrifyingly close now, yet still moving with excruciating slowness. McNally kept glancing over his shoulder, then returning to his struggle to free himself from the muck. I wondered if the ground was like that everywhere, or if he had just stepped into a particularly bad spot. I decided it must be the latter, since otherwise he would never have gotten that far from the gate.

I was trying to gauge the time it would take for the

monsters to reach him, when Beezle Whompis cried, "That's it! All right, come on over, Ronald."

I spun around.

Pleskit was holding a small, glittering device. It looked like a silver tennis ball with a couple dozen short purple pencils jabbed into its surface.

"See if you can carry this," said Barvgis. "Be careful — it's heavier than it looks."

The little mutant picked up the device. He staggered a bit under its weight but didn't fall.

Clearly Wiktor's boast that his mutating ray had given the hamsters superior strength had been true.

"I think we should strap it onto my back," said Ronald. "It will be easier for me to move that way."

Very quickly Pleskit and Barvgis used some cords to attach the device to Ronald's back, placing some padding under it so the pencil-like extensions would not poke him too badly.

When that was done, Barvgis handed Ronald a tightly folded piece of paper. "Here are the directions for using it," he said. "Give them to McNally."

"Will do," said Ronald stoutly. He raised his paw to his brow in a salute.

Aliens, Underwear, and Monsters

"It's going to be a terrifying task," warned Pleskit.

Ronald nodded and said simply, "I am ready to face my destiny."

"He's the bravest hamster I've ever met," murmured Rafaella as I carried Ronald to the oval of green light that still floated where McNally had disappeared.

"Good luck," I whispered.

"Thanks," said Ronald.

Then he turned and leaped from my hand into the opening.

CHAPTER 14

[PLESKIT]
HAZY, WITH A CHANCE OF INVASION

"Where is he?" said Tim. "What's happened to him?"

"He won't show up on the monitor right away," I said. "It's not focused on the exact place where he went through, so there's a blind spot for us. Besides, he's so small, we might not be able to see him at all through that mist."

A minute went by, then another.

Long minutes.

"Look!" cried Rafaella. "There he is!"

"Go, Ronald!" shouted Jordan, somewhat to my surprise. "Run, you crazy hamster. *Run!*"

Aliens, Underwear, and Monsters

Ronald was doing just that, scurrying across the strange landscape, leaping over knobs of ground, skirting the edges of bubbling pools of muck. Occasionally he would disappear into a swirl of mist, only to come darting out the other side of it a moment later.

"How can he go so fast?" asked Rafaella.

"Must be he's so light that the ground doesn't pull him down," I said.

Finally Ronald reached McNally's side. As we watched, he tugged on the leg of my bodyguard's trousers. McNally jumped, clearly startled, then smiled when he saw Ronald.

Ronald held up the device and the instructions. McNally began to read them. Time was getting short — the first of the slow monsters had almost reached him. McNally glanced over his shoulder, then turned his attention back to the paper.

"I can't believe he can stay so calm!" said Jordan, who was chewing the corner of his thumbnail.

I couldn't either. The monster had almost reached him. I think I would have done an accidental *finussher* by that point.

Suddenly McNally held up the device and began

to press the pencil-like protuberances. A bolt of blue-green energy exploded out of the thing. We staggered back as we heard a ripping sound in the air.

"It worked!" cried Rafaella.

Indeed it had. Shimmering in the center of the room was an oval of light, plenty large enough for McNally to come through.

We all began to cheer.

Then — disaster! The monster that had been lurching toward McNally grabbed him from behind. It pulled him right out of the clinging muck, unintentionally doing him a huge favor. McNally struggled and squirmed, managing to break free of the beast's huge arms. When McNally landed on the ground again, he began to hop about, though I couldn't tell if that was because he was doing Koo Muk Dwan moves or just trying to find a solid place to stand.

All of a sudden he dropped into a strange pose.

"I know that one!" cried Tim. "It's the Bam of Boo!"

Before the words were completely out of his mouth, McNally had launched himself forward. The monster swung a mighty blow at him. It was slow, but obviously incredibly powerful. McNally ducked the blow easily, then lashed out sideways with his foot.

The monster, which was at least three feet taller than McNally, staggered back.

"Look at Ronald!" cried Jordan.

The miniature mutant was leaping about. We couldn't hear him, of course, but he seemed to be screaming and shouting.

"He's trying to distract the monster," said Rafaella. "What a brave little hamster!"

What Ronald did next was even braver. After leaping onto the monster's ankle, he sank his teeth into its flesh!

"I hope he doesn't catch any weird extra-dimensional disease," said Rafaella uneasily.

The monster bent to look at Ronald. That was all McNally needed. One, two, three flashing Koo Muk Dwan moves, and the thing was staggering, reeling, ready to fall. And then — new disaster! As it toppled over, moving faster than it had ever managed to on its own, one of the monster's arms struck McNally on the side of his head. The monster hit the ground.

So did McNally.

He didn't move.

"He's been knocked out!" cried Tim in horror.

Ronald leaped off the monster's ankle and raced up its body to McNally. He tugged at his ear, then bent and yelled into it.

McNally didn't move.

And there were still two monsters coming!

"I'm going in," said Tim.

"What?" cried Rafaella.

"Someone has to go get McNally," said Tim. "He's my *geeba-raku*. Therefore, I'm the one to go."

"Tim is right," said Barvgis. "The only way to get McNally back is for someone to go after him. Beezle Whompis cannot pass through the gate. I would go, but I am not built for quick action. And we have no time to waste."

"Give me a ray gun," said Tim.

Barvgis shook his head. "We don't keep weapons in the embassy."

"Pansies," said Jordan in disgust.

Ignoring him, Tim nodded and said, "All right. I'm going anyway."

"Tim!" said Rafaella.

"What?"

Aliens, Underwear, and Monsters

She paused, then gave him a quick kiss on the cheek. "Good luck."

"Thanks," said Tim, with kind of a goofy smile. Then he turned and leaped through the oval of light.

I watched in admiration, wondering what it is that allows Earthlings to take such direct action in the face of physical danger, and feeling embarrassed that I find it so hard to act decisively in moments like that myself—though I had done it once, back on Geembol Seven.

"Where is he?" cried Rafaella. "What happened to him?"

Her question forced me to push aside my self-doubts. "He's in the blind spot," I said, turning my attention to the monitor. "He should show up soon."

But before Tim came into view, I suddenly spotted a new problem. *"Ziffl-pork,"* I muttered, making the small and rancid fart of fear.

"What?" asked Rafaella. "What is it?"

I pointed to the monitor. "There, off to the right. That monster—the tall reddish one with four arms. I think he's spotted the gateway."

This wasn't one of the monsters that had been

after McNally. It was another of the creatures that filled this weird dimension.

"He hasn't just spotted it," said Jordan in alarm. "He's coming right for it!"

I felt my *clinkus* tighten. "If he pushes his way through, he's going to show up right here — right in this room!"

"But we can't close the gate until Tim and McNally and Ronald get back," said Rafaella.

"Actually, I'm not sure we can close it at all," said Barvgis.

I looked at him in horror. "What are you talking about?"

Beezle Whompis crackled into sight. "Barvgis and I were in such a hurry to construct a device to open the gate that we didn't take the normal precautions. The very act of opening a two-way gate over an existing gate altered it so that it will not close automatically, as it normally would have. It may stay open forever."

I had to fight to keep from slipping into *kleptra*. "But if the monsters discover it, we could be facing a full-fledged invasion. They might overrun the planet! We've got to find a way to close it!"

Aliens, Underwear, and Monsters

"But not till the others get back," said Rafaella firmly.

"You're right," I said. "But that means we'd better be ready to face a monster if it comes through."

"Not if," said Jordan hoarsely. *"When!"*

He pointed to the monitor. The four-armed monster was terrifyingly close to the gate. Suddenly it disappeared. It had moved into the blind spot.

An instant later a horrible, groping arm thrust through the gate, its oozy fingers opening and closing as they searched for a victim.

CHAPTER 15

[TIM]
WEIRDNESS

When I first went through the dimensional gate, I felt as if I had been taken apart atom by atom, then put back together again. My body parts didn't seem to be connected the way they should be. The air, thick and hazy, swam in front of me. Clinging mists swirled around my feet. The surface I was standing on — I don't think you could really call it ground — wobbled under each step I took.

No wonder McNally had been dazed and confused when he'd gotten sucked into this place — especially since he hadn't been expecting it!

I stumbled forward, pulling my feet out of the

sucking, jiggling ground with each step. Then I found a patch of hard ground, which made things easier. Looking carefully, I noticed it was a slightly different color. I looked for another patch of the same color and moved toward it. Hard again!

Then one of the monsters yowled. Others answered it, like a chorus of dogs, except with sounds so spine-crawlingly weird that I could hardly move. Distracted and fearful, I didn't look carefully enough where I was going and tripped over an unexpected lump.

I fell flat on my face. But the ground was soft and cushiony, unexpectedly comfortable. The mist was surprisingly pleasant to breathe. Its strange aroma, spicy but appealing, filled my nostrils, relaxing me, relaxing me . . .

"Mmmmm," I murmured. "Smells good. *Feels* so nice and soft. Maybe I should take a little rest."

I closed my eyes.

I don't know how much time passed before I felt a tiny hand smacking me on the cheek. "Tim!" shrieked a little voice. "Tim, get up! Get up! You've got to help McNally!"

I blinked my eyes open. "What?" I looked around and realized where I was. How could I possibly have been about to go to sleep?

"I think there's something about that vapor that makes you want to sleep," said Ronald. "I'm lucky, it doesn't seem to affect me. But it hits humans hard. I can't get McNally up at all. The monster knocked him out, and he was down so long that I don't know if he'll ever wake up. Come on, come on, you've got to help me!"

Pushing myself to my feet was one of the hardest things I've ever done, worse than trying to drag yourself out of the deepest sleep you've ever been in. But once I was up and away from that spicy smell, it was a little easier.

I shook my head to clear it, slapped myself across the face a couple of times, then staggered toward McNally. Ronald, who had been clinging to my leg, scampered forward to check on him. "Hurry!" he cried, waving his tiny arms at me. "Hurry!"

But hurrying in the monster dimension was not easy for someone who wasn't tiny like Ronald. Being here was incredibly different from simply seeing it on the monitor. Now I was smelling it, hearing it, feeling

Aliens, Underwear, and Monsters

it—even tasting it, I realized, since the air itself was thick and sour on my tongue, oddly different from how it had been when I'd been lying on the ground, nearly asleep.

I saw a monster lumbering toward me, but it was moving so slowly that my first thought was it had no chance of catching me. Then I realized how slowly I was moving myself. The ground, or whatever I was walking on, was purple and mucky and seemed to want to suck me down. It was like being trapped in one of those dreams where you're trying to run but can't. I began to understand why the monsters all moved so slowly. I looked for more of the solid patches I had seen earlier, but couldn't find any.

It seemed like ages before I reached McNally, even though he wasn't that far away. The body of the monster he had knocked out was lying next to him, one arm flopped over his chest. I lifted the arm, hoping the monster wouldn't wake.

The green flesh was slick and flabby-feeling.

The monster snorted but didn't rouse.

Once I had its arm off McNally, I knelt beside him and pulled him to a sitting position, eager to get his head away from those treacherous vapors that made you sleepy.

"Come on, McNally," I said, shaking his shoulders. "Wake up. *Wake up!* We've got to get out of here!"

He groaned and opened his eyes. "Tim?" he said, sounding surprised. "What are you doing here?"

He glanced around. "And where the heck is 'here,' anyway?" Suddenly his eyes widened. "Wait, I'm starting to remember. Holy cow! We've got to get moving! *Fast!*"

"Fast won't be easy," I said. "Everything seems to go slowly here."

"Well, slow beats standing still," he said. "Come on, before my buddy here starts to wake up."

I helped him to his feet, but as I did, he staggered and nearly fell again. "My leg!" he said, gritting his teeth in pain. "There's something wrong with my leg!"

"Can you walk at all?" I asked.

"I'm going to need to lean on you."

"No problem," I said, not entirely truthfully. "Let's go."

We started off again, McNally using me for support. But the two monsters were getting closer, drooling and grunting as they made their slow way toward

us. More than ever I wished that I had a ray gun, since I would rather stun them than injure them. But I figured if it came right down to it, it was better them than us, so I turned to McNally and said, "Maybe you should use your gun."

"I'm not carrying a gun," he said.

I looked at him in astonishment. "But you're a bodyguard!"

"Yeah, when I'm out in the world. But I'm off duty when we're in the embassy, because it's supposed to be secure."

"We'd better move faster," I said. Wrapping my arm around him so I could take more of his weight, I started slogging toward the dimensional gate. It shimmered invitingly in front of us, but inviting as it was, I mostly looked down, trying not to trip or fall in any of the holes.

"Oh, cripe," muttered McNally a moment later.

"What?" I asked. At the same time, I looked up. To my horror, a monster had thrust its arm right through the gate and was trying to climb in ahead of us.

"We have to go faster!" said McNally.

But that wasn't possible. The thick, clinging,

mucky ground — the dimension itself — seemed to be trying to hold us down. To make things worse, some of the monsters seemed to have taken our attempt to escape as an invitation to attack. They were shambling toward us, faster than I had yet seen them move.

The closest was a huge and hideous creature with three enormous eyes and a lower lip that dangled past its chin. I glanced over my shoulder and realized it was only a few feet away. Desperate, I began fishing in my backpack for something, anything, I could use as a weapon.

The first thing I found was my boxer shorts, which were still where I had stuffed them after the flagpole incident.

So I did the only thing I could think of.

I threw my underwear at the monster.

The creature snatched them out of the air and began to examine them, looking at them as if they were the strangest things he had ever seen. He held them up and began to sniff at them.

Then he put them on his head.

Great — this was the second alien to be in that

underwear in one day! I decided I probably wasn't going to wear them anymore, even if I did get them back.

McNally and I staggered another few steps forward. The monsters were getting closer.

"Tim, watch out!" cried Ronald, who was still clinging to my leg.

I turned to look over my shoulder. One of the monsters was closer than ever— close enough to reach me. And he was stretching his arm toward me.

It was Koo Muk Dwan time!

CHAPTER 16

[PLESKIT]
GAS ATTACK

The sight of that monster's arm waving around as it tried to push its way into the embassy finally forced me into action. I grabbed a metal measuring rod from the lab table and began to beat at the grasping hand.

It did no good. The monster seized the rod and wrenched it from my hands, sending me thudding against the wall as it did. Then it began to swing the rod around, making it impossible for us to get close.

Soon the creature had forced its way through the opening. It had scaly, purple-red skin and a goggle-eyed face. Fierce-looking horns covered its head and shoulders. Its fingers—three on each hand—ended in sharp black claws. Two thick fangs curved up from its lower jaw. It was drooling—a thick, acid-smelling ooze that dripped from its dangling lower lip and sizzled when it hit the floor.

"You get back to where you came from!" cried Beebo. At the same time, he began using his telekinetic powers to fling at the creature all the loose pieces of lab equipment that he could find.

The monster ignored the barrage of items.

Suddenly I heard a deep, rumbling voice roar, "Creeaadllll-gaaaahhhh!"

It was the battle cry of Barvgis! The faithful slime-ball came lumbering forward, using his mighty girth to try to force the monster back. The creature seemed startled that anyone would dare attempt such a thing. Roaring back, it pushed at Barvgis.

He was immovable.

The monster began to beat on him.

Barvgis's thick flesh absorbed the blows. I knew they must hurt, but Barvgis stood firm.

Then the creature slashed at him with its claws, opening three wide gashes. Barvgis cried out in startled pain and staggered backward, clapping his hand over the wounds.

I thought his retreat would give the creature free access, but Beezle Whompis flickered into sight right in front of it, crackling with furious energy.

The creature's googly eyes widened, and it lurched back.

Beezle Whompis vanished, reappeared just as quickly, then vanished again. For a moment, his strategy seemed to be working. But after the third reappearance the creature got used to the effect. Growling and thrashing its thick arms, it pressed forward again.

Jordan, Rafaella, and I were crouched under the lab table. I do not want to sound like a coward, but sometimes it makes sense to fight, and sometimes it is better to hide. None of us was prepared to battle a monster like this.

Despite his wounds, Barvgis flung himself into the fray again. The monster locked its arms around him and began to squeeze. This turned out to be a mistake for the monster, because it squeezed so hard that Barvgis belched in its face.

The belch, a long and mighty masterpiece, caused the monster to shriek and try to pull back.

Barvgis wouldn't let go. Realizing how the monster was reacting, he locked his own arms around it and belched again.

The monster wailed in despair, a sound that made my guts grind.

"It doesn't like gas!" cried Rafaella.

"Try a fart, Pleskit!" urged Jordan. "Try a fart!"

I hurried to Barvgis's side, turned my back, and closed my eyes. Gathering all my strength, I squinched my eyes shut, tugged on my *sphen-gnut-ksher,* and summoned the horrible fart of righteous indignation.

CHAPTER 17

[TIM]
TRAPPED

As I dropped into a protective crouch, I tried to remember all the moves McNally had taught me during our training sessions. I had been learning the art for a pathetically short time, but my *geeba-raku* was a good teacher.

And the monsters, horrible as they were, had no training at all! I lunged at the closest one, slashing at it with my hands as I uttered the Cry of the Angry Gazelle.

It lurched back, looking astonished. I couldn't tell if this was because I had created fear, which was the point, or if it was simply amazed someone so small would dare try to fight it.

Aliens, Underwear, and Monsters

"Use the Hands of Suzy Kwan!" said McNally, who had fallen again when I'd let go of him. He was holding himself up on his elbows, to keep his face out of the sleep-inducing vapors.

I pressed forward, slashing at the monster.

It whimpered and turned to flee — which, of course, it couldn't do very fast.

"Nice work," said Ronald, who had jumped down from my leg and was standing on McNally's shoe.

Before I could feel any pride, I was grabbed from behind by yet another of the beasts.

"Quick, Tim, use the Mr. Moto Mojo Move!" ordered McNally, as if we were still back in the embassy gym and this were nothing but training.

Without even having to think, I bent forward. Letting the monster's own weight do most of the work, I sent the creature flying over my shoulder. It crashed to the jellylike ground, creating a ripple that nearly knocked me off my feet.

Another monster pressed forward. It almost managed to get me in its grip, but suddenly Ronald leaped onto its leg. As I was trying to fight the monster, the little mutant scurried right up the creature's side.

When he reached the monster's shoulder, Ronald put his face right next to its ear—which was about the same size as Ronald—and shouted, "Leave my friend alone, you big lummox!"

The monster looked totally astonished.

Ronald began gnawing on its ear.

The monster cried out and moved an arm toward its head. On Earth it would have been too fast for me to catch and might have smashed Ronald flat. But I had time to grab the creature. Turning its energy against itself with the Grasshopper Meets the Gorilla, I flipped the monster backward.

Ronald jumped away and came scampering back to me.

The other monsters started to back away from us.

"Let's get going!" I said.

Squatting down, I got McNally's arm around my shoulders, and helped him to his feet again. We began lurching forward. The monsters watched warily but seemed to be holding back, not sure what to make of us.

We're going to make it! I thought. *We're going to make it!*

Aliens, Underwear, and Monsters

Then, just when the gate was almost in reach, Ronald fell into a hole. I saw him fall, heard a little shriek . . . then nothing.

At the same time, I heard the monsters begin moving forward again, heard the slow sucking sound they made as their feet pulled out of the jellylike ground.

Step by horrible step they were moving toward us.

The dimensional gate was just a few feet ahead. I longed to press on, to break free of this horrible place.

But I couldn't leave Ronald.

He's just a hamster, I told myself. *There are two human lives at stake here.* But I couldn't convince myself of that. I knew Ronald was far more than a hamster. And he had not worried about his own safety when he'd come through the gate to help McNally.

I glanced over my shoulder. The monsters were moving, but they were as slow as ever. I had time.

I made my choice. Pressing on to the dimensional gate, I thrust McNally through.

Then I turned and headed back for Ronald.

There's time, I told myself, over and over again. *Those monsters are at least ten feet back. Maybe fifteen. And they're moving slowly. I'm faster than they are. I can save Ronald, get us both out of here. I know I can.*

By the time I had finished giving myself this pep talk, I had made it back to the hole where Ronald had vanished. Taking a deep breath so that I wouldn't have to breathe any of the dangerous sleeping vapor, I knelt and thrust my hand into the hole.

I had to reach in past my elbow before I felt his little body. It was warm, which was a relief, but he wasn't moving. With a little work, I managed to scoop him into my palm. But when I tried to pull him out of the hole, the ground locked around me, as if the world itself were planning to swallow me.

I struggled to pull free, but the more I fought, the tighter the ground seemed to hold me.

CHAPTER 18

[RAFAELLA]
TUG-OF-WAR

Pleskit's fart was horrifying, but it sent the monster reeling backward, clawing at its face and screeching as if it were trapped in some terrible nightmare.

"Do it again, Pleskit!" shouted Jordan from where the two of us were hiding under the table. "Do it again!"

Pleskit did.

The monster yelped in horror. Clutching its face, it burst into tears. Then it turned and plunged back toward the dimensional gate. But it was not an easy fit; the beast got stuck halfway through. Barvgis ran forward and gave it a firm push from behind, then rubbed his hands in satisfaction as it popped through.

For a moment—just a moment—I felt an enormous sense of relief. And some frustration, too. I would have liked to help. But what could I have done? I suspected Jordan was feeling the same way, except probably even more so, since he's a guy.

I crawled out from under the table and looked at the monitor to see if I could find Tim. He was supporting McNally as the two of them struggled their way across the weird, jellylike ground. I could see more monsters behind them, but they were moving slowly, and it looked as if Tim and McNally would make it.

Then Ronald fell into a hole!

I could tell Tim knew it had happened, because he hesitated. Then he continued on toward the gate. I was furious. How could he leave Ronald behind?

Tim and McNally disappeared from sight as they reached the blind spot close to the gate. A moment later McNally came stumbling into the lab. He collapsed to the floor, clutching his leg.

"Oh, man, we made it," he said. "Well done, Tim. Tim? TIM?"

Aliens, Underwear, and Monsters

"He's not here," said Pleskit.

McNally pushed himself up on one arm, still clutching his leg with the other. "Where is he?"

"He went back to get Ronald!" I cried, feeling so proud of him, I thought I might burst.

We watched the monitor eagerly as Tim slogged back to where Ronald had disappeared — actually slogged *toward* some of the monsters. But when he plunged his arm into the ground to try to get Ronald, he got stuck. I could see him struggling to get free. I could also see the monsters moving slowly but surely in his direction.

Something inside me snapped. Without stopping to think, I flung myself at the dimensional gate. A tingle, a blur of colors, a sudden burst of pain — and then I was standing in a place so strange that I realized for the first time that going through the gate was not merely like going to another planet.

I had gone to another *reality*!

The weirdness made me stagger. My stomach lurched, and I nearly threw up.

"Rafaella!" cried Tim when he saw me. "What are you doing here?"

"I came to get you," I said, starting toward him.

"Go back while you still can!" he cried. I could hear the fear in his voice, but it didn't make me think he was a coward. He was right to be afraid in this place. And he had already proved his bravery.

"We'll go back together," I said, struggling to walk on the wobbling ground. It was like trying to walk through Jell-O. "As soon as we get you and Ronald loose."

"I don't think that's going to happen," said Tim, his voice thick with fear. "My arm is stuck." He paused, then

Aliens, Underwear, and Monsters

added, "I'm not even sure Ronald's still alive. I almost think the ground is trying to . . . to *eat* us."

That was the moment when the energy that had sent me bursting through the gate vanished. In its place came a flood of fear. How could I have been so stupid? What had I been thinking of, to throw myself into this other dimension, this world of monsters?

Shut up! I told that part of my brain. *I'm helping a friend. That's not stupid!*

It is if you both end up dead, replied the scared part of my brain.

Well, it's too late to worry about that now, I argued back. *Now we just have to figure a way out of here.*

The scared part shut up, which was just as well, since it didn't seem to have anything useful to say. When I finally made it to Tim, I knelt and tried to free his arm. I pulled on it. I tried clawing at the ground. I shouted and beat at it.

Nothing happened.

Finally I got behind Tim, grabbed him around the waist, and began to pull.

He was still stuck fast.

"Come on, Tim," I shouted. "Pull! *Pull!*"

I glanced up.

The monsters were getting closer. One of them was wearing Tim's underwear on its head.

Suddenly I felt someone grab me around the waist. I screamed.

"Be quiet," said a familiar voice. "Just keep pulling."

It was Jordan.

We pulled. It was like a tug-of-war, with Jordan, me, and Tim linked together trying to pull Ronald out of the ground as if he were a turnip or something.

"It's working!" cried Tim suddenly. "I can feel the ground loosening!"

A moment later we tumbled backward in a pile.

"Do you still have him?" I cried. "Do you still have Ronald?"

"Right here!" said Tim, holding up his hand. "Come on, let's get going!"

"But is he all right?" I struggled to my feet and grabbed Tim's arm.

Ronald was in his hand. I gasped. The little hamsteroid's eyes were closed, and he wasn't breathing.

Aliens, Underwear, and Monsters

"Ronald!" I cried. "Speak to me!"

No answer.

I snatched his limp body from Tim. "Breathe!" I cried, poking Ronald's chest with my fingertip, trying to CPR him back to life. "Come on, Ronald, *breathe!*"

No answer.

"We've got to get going, Raf," said Jordan, his voice surprisingly gentle. "We won't be able to do *anything* for Ronald if the monsters catch us."

I glanced over my shoulder. The monsters were almost on us, the one in Tim's underwear closest of all. Before I could say anything, Tim slogged forward. He was moving faster than the monsters, though not by a great deal, and seemed to be choosing the places he stepped. When he reached the closest monster, the one wearing his underwear, he jumped up and grabbed the edge of the waistband.

Then he pulled it down to cover the monster's eyes.

The monster roared in anger. The other monsters began making a strange sound. It took me a moment to realize it was laughter. To my astonishment, instead of helping their fellow monster, they began beating on him. The first monster wrenched Tim's boxer shorts off its head and began using them to smack the other monsters.

The boys and I turned and started back toward the dimensional gate, Ronald's still, quiet body cradled in my hands.

CHAPTER 19

[PLESKIT]
BEEBO DOES HIS BIT

We watched breathlessly as Tim, Rafaella, and Jordan made their way toward the dimensional gate. When they entered the blind spot, I felt a surge of fear because I couldn't see them — combined with a rush of hope because they were so close.

A moment later they were back in the lab. Rafaella immediately slumped to the floor and began to work on Ronald's tiny body, pumping his chest with her fingertip and whispering, "Breathe! Come on, Ronald, breathe. Please breathe!"

Tim came to stand next to me. "Can we put him on the Heal-a-tron?" he asked softly.

"We'd have to calibrate it properly," I said. "I don't think it has a setting for mutant hamsters."

"Shrink me!" demanded Rafaella suddenly.

"What?" I asked.

"Shrink me!" she cried, looking up from where she was crouched over Ronald. "Then I can give him mouth-to-mouth resuscitation! It might be his only hope!"

I raced to the Fatherly One's office to get the shrinking ray that had caused Tim and me so much trouble shortly after I had arrived on the planet. When I got back to the lab, I set the ray so it would shrink Rafaella to about eight inches—small enough for her to give Ronald the breathing treatment, but not as violent a transition as the one Tim and Ms. Weintraub had gone through when they'd shrunk to two inches. I calculated that the shrinking would last about two hours.

The eight-inch-tall Rafaella was soon kneeling beside Ronald and breathing into his mouth.

"That is so gross," said Jordan, making a face.

Tim turned to him, and I could tell he was on the edge of making a sharp remark. Then he paused. I could see him trying to get control of himself. He took a deep breath, then said, "Thanks."

Aliens, Underwear, and Monsters

Jordan looked at him in surprise.

"For coming through to help get me back."

Jordan's surprise turned to embarrassment. "Hey, just 'cause you're a weenie doesn't mean I want to see you eaten by a monster," he said.

"Well, if you don't want to see anyone eaten by monsters, we'd better do something quick," said McNally, who was still lying on the floor. "That gate hasn't been closed yet."

"And the monsters that were after you three have stopped fighting," added Beezle Whompis, his voice crackling out of the air. "I've been watching the monitor while the rest of you were worrying about Ronald. One of them just ate Tim's boxer shorts."

"Great," said Tim. "This morning I had an alien in my underwear. Now my underwear is in an alien!"

"I wouldn't worry about that so much," said Beezle Whompis. "The bigger problem is that they're heading our way again!"

"Is there any way we can close the gate?" I asked.

"A burst of raw energy might do it," said Barvgis.

"You mean electricity?" asked Tim.

"No, we'd need a more pure form of power," said

Beezle Whompis, flickering briefly into sight.

"How about one of those energy snacks?" asked Beebo.

"That just might do it!" cried Barvgis.

From the air beside me came a crackling sound that I recognized as Beezle Whompis sighing over the loss of his last snack.

"It would have to strike the exact center of the gateway at very high speed to work," said Barvgis.

"I can do that," said Beebo confidently.

"I'll get it," I said. "Are they still on your desk, Beezle Whompis?"

"*It* is still there," he said. "The last one."

Once again, I hurried to the office area. I returned moments later, clutching the bag.

"Just set it down," said Beebo.

As soon as I had, he used his telekinetic powers to open the top of the bag. An instant later the glowing sphere floated out. When it moved to the back of the room, I wondered what Beebo was doing. Then I realized that he needed to get the sphere far enough away from the gate that he could build up some speed before it struck.

Aliens, Underwear, and Monsters

"Now!" said Beezle Whompis.

Beebo closed his eyes and tightened his little orange fists. The energy snack hurtled toward the dimensional gate. But just as it was about to strike, one of the monsters thrust its arm through the gate and began groping around.

"Avert!" shouted Barvgis desperately. "Avert!"

Beebo made a pained little cry. The energy snack swerved left and circled away from the opening. At the same instant Tim let out a terrible shriek. Leaping forward, he gave the huge arm two quick slashes with his hands.

The arm withdrew.

Beebo sent the energy snack toward the gate again. This time it shot forward and struck in the exact center.

I staggered back, flinging up my arms to cover my eyes as a dazzling blast of blue light filled the room.

CHAPTER 20

[TIM]
PEST RETRIEVAL SERVICE

I let out a whoop of delight. The dimensional gate had vanished! We all began to shout and cheer.

"Well done, Beebo!" I shouted, momentarily forgetting what a pest he was.

Then I realized that one person wasn't cheering. It was Rafaella, who was still kneeling beside Ronald, trying to breathe life into his little body. I knelt too — carefully, since Rafaella was only eight inches tall herself.

The others fell silent.

We all stared, holding our breath ourselves as we waited to see if Ronald would breathe again.

Aliens, Underwear, and Monsters

I was closest, so I was the one who saw it when his eyes fluttered open.

"Yes!" I cried, leaping to my feet and pumping my arm. "Yes, he's going to live!"

We began shouting and cheering again, thumping one another on the back. I found myself hugging Jordan, though that only lasted a second, because we both jumped back in shock and dismay.

Suddenly the door to the room slid open. For a second time, our cheering ground to a sudden halt.

Standing in the opening was Sookutan Krimble, Beebo's mentor/relative. Tall and dignified, *yeeble* had a look on *yeeble*'s face that was enough to make me tremble, even though it was clearly directed at Beebo.

Sookutan Krimble didn't say a word, just made a commanding gesture, then pointed to the floor beside *yeeble*. Beebo was standing there almost instantly. He looked so terrified, I almost felt sorry for him—which I must say I think was pretty big of me, all things considered.

Frek Krimble gazed around at the rest of us. "I see things have been . . . busy. I hope my rebellious *kribbl-pam* has not caused you too much trouble." Looking down at Beebo, *yeeble* added, "He has certainly brought trouble onto himself. This visit was unauthorized, and he will be severely punished for it."

Beebo twisted his hands and looked extremely embarrassed. "I just wanted to see my friends," he muttered.

Sookutan Krimble looked at him skeptically.

"Well, I also needed to get the diary I left behind. It was part of an assignment, and my teachercreature was very upset with me for not having it when I got back. Besides, I thought you would be very happy if I retrieved the body suit that I had left with Tim." He dropped to his knees and threw his arms around Sookutan Krimble's legs. "Please don't be mad at me!" he cried. "Please, please, please, please, please!"

Sookutan Krimble said nothing, but I could tell *yeeble* was trying not to smile.

"Beebo has indeed caused quite a bit of trouble, *Frek* Krimble," said Pleskit. "However, he has also redeemed himself in the last few minutes by cleverly helping to bring that same trouble to an end."

Sookutan Krimble nodded. "I will need details of

what he has done here," *yeeble* said. "A true and complete report will be necessary."

Beebo looked at us, and I could see his lips form two words: "Have mercy!"

The annoying thing was, I knew we probably would.

CHAPTER 21

[PLESKIT]
A LETTER HOME

FROM: Pleskit Meenom, on the bizarre but always fascinating Planet Earth
TO: Maktel Geebrit, on the beloved and much-missed Planet Hevi-Hevi

Dear Maktel,

Well, there you have it—the complete story of yet another near-catastrophe from our outpost here on Earth.

Beebo did take his body suit and diary when he returned to Roogbat. *Frek* Krimble continued to pretend to be angry, but to tell the truth, I do not think the little pest will be punished very severely. The *Frek yeebleself* remained for another day to consult with the Fatherly One. I am very curious about what they are up to, but the Fatherly One has not seen fit to explain their plans to me.

Rafaella soon returned to her normal size, of course. And we were able to calibrate the Heal-a-tron to work on McNally, so his leg was quickly back in working order, which was a relief, since I have come to rely on his protection.

As for Doris, she has still not been captured. So I go to school every day knowing I have a tiny enemy lurking in the walls. It is not a comfortable feeling.

I wonder what you think when you read these things, Maktel. Do you wish you could be here to share in the action? Or do the stories make you thankful that you are safe and sound on Hevi-Hevi?

Ms. Weintraub likes to say that adventures are always more fun to read about than to live through. I am beginning to believe that this is true.

Aliens, Underwear, and Monsters

But it's not just the danger that bothers me these days. What is even worse is the fact that nothing is solid now. Everything seems about to change and shift. Sixth grade will soon be coming to an end. At the same time, the Fatherly One is facing enormous challenges regarding our mission. What will the next months bring? Will the Fatherly One's peaceful mission thrive? Will we become fabulously wealthy? Or will we lose everything in some scandal cooked up by our enemies—or, even worse, because of some foolish mistake I make that creates more trouble here on Earth?

If we do fail, I shudder to think of what will happen to the Earthlings if one of the other Traders waiting in line takes over the franchise.

The odd thing is, I do not care anymore if we become rich. I just want to live the way we used to before the Fatherly One became so important. I liked life better when he had time to spend with me.

Sometimes I long to be back on Hevi-Hevi. Other times I wonder if my time here on Earth has changed me so much that I would no longer fit in at home.

Please write soon, Maktel. I miss hearing from you, from a place where everything makes sense.

Fremmix Bleeblom!

Your confused pal,

Pleskit

P.S.: I am still not certain what is going on with Ralph-the-Driver. I have watched but have not seen him flip that switch again. But that might be because he *knows* I am watching him. I will let you know if I figure anything out.

A GLOSSARY OF ALIEN TERMS

Following are definitions for alien words and phrases appearing for the first time in *Aliens, Underwear, and Monsters.* The number after a definition indicates the chapter where the word first appeared.

For most words, we only give the spelling. In actual usage, of course, many Hevi-Hevian words are accompanied by smells and/or body sounds.

Definitions of other extraterrestrial words appearing in this book can be found in the volumes of the Sixth-Grade Alien series where they were first used.

FOOJSTAD: An environmental catastrophe. The word derives from the Fooj, a strange species of birdlike creatures found on Moorkbo Three. The Fooj created ever-expanding nests by continually accumulating things they found that appealed to them. The nests would eventually collapse, often killing the inhabitants.

The Fooj are now extinct, a fate that surprised none of the biologists who studied them. (6)

GUKSTET: Earlenmeyer Gukstet, a Trader scientist from Frobitz Eleven who did much of the early work on interdimensional viewing. He disappeared mysteriously at the height of his career, and there have been (at last count) 2,148 poems, 48 novels, 7 operas, and 118 tri-D presentations contemplating his fate. (4)

KEEKLE-BOONGERS: Literally "delighters of my emotional being." A term of endearment often used by parental units for their younglings, or between beings who are becoming mating partners, or by pet owners for their animal companions. (The correct plural would actually be *keekle-boongerri*, of course, but in using the word in an English sentence, Shhh-foop has adapted the English method of forming plurals.) (11)

KLOOPENZOOFERS: A salty-sweet snack made from living honey, fermented *dweezil* beans, and *plonkus* blubber. The appealing glow comes from the interaction of the *dweezil* beans and the honey. *Kloopenzoo-ferri* (again, Shhh-foop is using a corrupted plural) are often used as good-night snacks for children afraid of the dark. (11)

Aliens, Underwear, and Monsters

SPOOBERGORT: A highly vulgar exclamation of dismay. (13)

ZIFFL-PORK: Lingtram Ziffl was founder of a gloomy school of philosophy known as the Sporgstad Doomsayers. This group believed that no matter how bad things were, they were bound to get worse. When hundreds of years of continuous progress and improvement finally convinced them they were wrong, the group disbanded, leaving only the phrase coined from their founder's name, *ziffl-pork*. The term, still uttered in times of despair, is usually taken to mean "Just when you thought things couldn't get worse, here we go again!" (14)